MW01030883

Mulberry Street Stories

ALSO BY MARY MCLAUGHLIN SLECHTA

POETRY

Wreckage on a Watery Moon

The Boy's Nightmare and Other Poems

Love and Other Strangers

Buried Bones

FICTION

The Spoonmaker's Diamond: A Chooseable Path Novel for Learning English Expressions

Mulberry Street Stories

MARY MCLAUGHLIN SLECHTA

FOUR WAY
TRIBECA

Copyright 2023 Mary McLaughlin Slechta

No part of this book may be used or reproduced in any manner without written permission except in the case of brief quotations embodied in critical articles and reviews.

LIBRARY OF CONGRESS CATALOGING-IN-PUBLICATION DATA

Names: Slechta, Mary McLaughlin, 1956- author.

Title: Mulberry Street stories / by Mary McLaughlin Slechta.

Identifiers: LCCN 2023004451 (print) | LCCN 2023004452 (ebook)

| ISBN 9781954245747 (trade paperback) | ISBN 9781954245754 (ebook)

Subjects: LCGFT: Poetry.

Classification: LCC PS3619.L424 2023 (print) | LCC PS3619.L424 2023

  (ebook) | DDC 811/.6--dc23/eng/20230317

LC record available at https://lccn.loc.gov/2023004451

LC ebook record available at https://lccn.loc.gov/2023004452

This book is manufactured in the United States of America and printed on acid-free paper.

Four Way Books is a not-for-profit literary press. We are grateful for the assistance we receive from individual donors, public arts agencies, and private foundations including the NEA, and the New York State Council on the Arts, a state agency.

We are a proud member of the Community of Literary Magazines and Presses.

FOR MOM

CONTENTS

Mulberry Street Stories

A HOUSE ON MULBERRY STREET

Even before Dessa's father pulled the fish fully out of the water, he was telling her about luck and being lucky. All because he had caught a carp, long and silvery wonderful in the sunlight.

"It's too big for the bucket," he shouted. Running to the truck for a knife to scale and gut it on the spot, he told her to mind the fish didn't get away.

That was easier said than done for a lucky fish is a wily one. As soon as he was gone, it wheezed and spit and found its proper voice.

"Little girl," it said. "Your father has promised you one of my scales for luck. I offer you much more if you let me go."

Dessa's head came closer, the better to hear, but her feet stayed back.

"Don't be afraid," it said. "Your father is a small man compared to the fine woman you are meant to be. Tip over the bucket so I can return to the lake, then refill it and tell him the fish flew away."

"He won't believe me."

But when the carp promised her three wishes, she did as she was told.

The lie was useless. Her father hit her hard enough to make her ears ring. "There went my luck," he groaned. "Gray days and cold nights ahead. Empty bellies. An early grave for your mother, the jailhouse for me, and bad teeth all around. The house will burn to the ground and your grandmother will return from the dead and tell where I buried her money in the yard." He raised his hand to hit her again.

"I wish you wouldn't," Dessa sobbed.

3

Finding his hand frozen midair, he swung a leg to kick her, and again she sobbed, "I wish you wouldn't."

So there he stood, trying to balance on one foot, when the carp rose from the water, thick as an elephant and long as the road that runs from the city into the country. It did indeed have wings.

"Poor Dessa!" it exclaimed. "You've wasted two wishes on a fool. What will you wish for now?"

"For me," snapped the fisherman. "She'll wish me back to the man I was."

Dessa shivered at the thought and said, "I wish—"

"Yes," said the carp.

"Quickly," said her father.

"I wish for a house on Mulberry Street."

"Now who's the fool?" Her father, laughing bitterly, tumbled into the reeds where you'll find him still.

As for a house on Mulberry Street, it's a fine wish. The houses are sturdy as castles and the neighbors, who walk about as kings and queens, will deign to push you out of the snowbanks and bring you pie and if you've been housebound bellow a "Happy New Year" well into spring and in June honk at you and your friends in your caps and gowns. Good people. The best. Oh, to be loved like that.

Dessa, her mother, and grandmother lived there happily for many years.

THE PICKLED NEGRO

Normally Ola came straight home from the bus stop, but as there had been a string of yard sales over the weekend, she meandered to see what treasures had gone unsold. In the first house she found an unchipped teacup among a shattered dinner service and a ceramic cat that would look fine on her windowsill. It would be nice to have the company. She found other interesting things at the next house, but the tabletop was warped, the chair missing an arm, and a pretty wicker basket was without a bottom. The cat, when she checked again, had only one ear, so she put it on the chair's remaining arm. She thought of tea in her new cup and hurried along until she spotted a clay pickle crock outside the third house. *The Ward Wellington Ward.*

Ward Wellington Ward, in all bold print on the flyers, had meant nothing last spring until she wandered into the Open House. She helped herself to coffee and a molasses cookie while other visitors chattered about the craftsman style. *Impeccably built, beautifully maintained—Ward Wellington Ward* meant fine taste and money. She normally resented white people talking down to her about things they presumed she'd never own, but the dark, well-oiled wood throughout the house made her a dark, well-oiled child again, silent under the pressure of her mother's hands on a Sunday morning. She gingerly tried out one of the *Stickley* chairs.

"You look like you belong here," the agent said, and she felt herself flush.

The pickle crock seemed to be in perfect condition. She glanced at the Sold sign in the yard, then the closed shutters. No one living there.

She tried to check inside the crock, but the wooden lid was stuck. She strained to lift it. Took a few steps. Set it down. Lifted. Walked. Set it down. Rolled it a few feet. In this way she was home in forty minutes instead of the usual five. When she got to the front steps and sat down, her racing heart scared her. She pressed her hands to her head and prayed the throbbing would stop.

One of the drug dealers, his pants hung low, came out of the house across the street, probably headed for the corner. He pulled his head in and out of his neck a few times before he made a sharp turn onto the middle of the street, a turkey pretending not to see her through his squinty eyes. He walked past like he was too busy, too important, to ask a middle-aged neighbor if she was okay. Someone who knew his grandmother and knew him too, before she didn't.

"Trifling," she muttered to herself. "If I could just sell out . . . ."

When the pickle crock finally sat in the middle of the kitchen floor, her exhaustion turned to excitement. Didn't old people hide money in strange places? She ran a butter knife around the rim until there was a whoop of escaping air, followed by a disappointing whiff of vinegar and pickling spice. A second later, her imagination having shifted to a bag of rare coins stashed in brine, she lifted the lid and nearly fell backwards with fright. Two brown palms lay flat above a head of matted hair. She squinted at a leather tag placed neatly between the hands. *Pickled Negro.*

shh-loop

The brine began to bubble, and the thing inside, surely it couldn't be human, or alive, shifted and expanded as though filling with air.

shh-loop

shh-loop

She held the knife defensively against her chest, immobile as fingers wriggled free from the brine and rose like pale, undulating sea creatures with long accordion-like bodies. Arms. At their full length, the scrawny limbs reached back to the crock where the palms, anchoring themselves to the rim, began to push . . . and push . . . torturously birthing a shriveled head and shoulders, then a sticky torso with breasts so mal-formed and shriveled that it was impossible to tell if this were a man or woman.

There was a suspension of activity as the creature's eyes blinked open. It seemed to be testing its mouth and nose before pushing again, this time pulling out one sticky foot, then the other. When it stood upright in tattered trousers held together by a thin rope, its skin had already dried to a greenish shade of ash. A man! The top of his head barely reached her hip.

Leprechaun, she decided. The tag a bluff because leprechauns are known tricksters, and there is no such thing as a *Pickled Negro*. Especially not in a *Ward Wellington Ward* house.

"You owe me a wish," she told it. "A wish for freeing you from the pickle crock."

The leprechaun met her gaze with an expression of surprise, then throwing back its head and giving a snort of indignation, doubled over, coughing brine on her clean floor before it spoke.

"I ain't stayed pickled this long to be spoke to so. And by someone black as you."

She was outraged by the racist Irishman.

"Keep talking," she threatened, stabbing the air with the knife. "Fool, you owe me a pot of gold."

"Then I reckon you the fool."

The two faced each other down for several minutes during which Ola chided herself for being baited by a . . . She reappraised the deep carv-ings in the face and thought of the wooden craftsmanship in the *Ward Wellington Ward*. Perhaps it wasn't a leprechaun but something more rare. More valuable. An animatron made out of wood and mechanical parts. The laughter, the voice, almost but not quite human.

She knew about them from TV and guessed this might be the first discovered in a pickle crock. Something so rare and so valuable, she wouldn't need to wish. She hoped it hadn't lost much value by being unsealed. The brine had greyed the surface but surely, with oiling, it could be darkened to its natural shade. The battery, or whatever it was that controlled language, was intact. And its motions, although choppy, very humanlike. Now it dropped its eyes in defeat. Now it shuffled its feet.

"Well, what you pay for old Roscoe?"

Hmpf! An animatron made to shuck and jive. A racist toy. She quickly recalculated. Black collectibles were hot right now, and not only because of white collectors. There were as many reasons as collectors. Like those Mammy salt and pepper shakers, not her thing but valuable to someone. *Hmmm.* She couldn't resist having a little fun. It was a toy after all.

"Didn't pay a cent. Not a rusty dime. Which makes the having all the better, don't you think?"

When it glanced up a moment, mockery flashing across its face, she stiffened. Didn't like it meeting her eye. Not one bit. It made her think how objects took on the spirit of their previous owners. The Raggedy Ann of a dead child. A bike, a bat, a ball—a haunting! She didn't believe in hauntings but she would sell it quick to have it out of the house. It was dangerous.

The thing seemed to sense her fear and tried to allay it by groveling, except she caught an undercurrent of scorn.

"Missus, is it true you ain't paid nuttin for Old Roscoe?"

Was it implying she had no right owning what was left on the curb to take? That she hadn't worked on getting it here for the past hour? It couldn't. Animatrons were probably like those Magic 8 Balls that only appeared to have a ready answer for your questions.

"I'll tell you what," she told the dumb thing. "My back will pay tomorrow from carrying you, so I *'spect* you owe me."

"I'se sorry, Missus. Most sorry Old Roscoe ain't got nuttin to give."

Could it hear itself? Of course not. Its fake humility was embarrassing. A minstrel show. Unable to stop herself, she continued to play along.

"Well, listen good Old Roscoe. Iffen you ain't got nuttin to give, how bouts I sell you?"

The change was immediate. Its whole body began to shake, its white lips flapping as if exposure to the air was destroying what the brine had preserved. Falling to the floor the thing clawed at her ankles, whimpering and begging. So pathetic and awful, so dirty and low, she wanted to smash it to bits.

A *Pickled Negro*? Who would create such a monster? She wouldn't sell it. Couldn't. Not for any amount of money give a white collector a chuckle at her expense. Laying aside the knife, she took up a hammer from the drawer. But as she made ready to strike, to remove it from her kitchen and the world, it froze. Where were the hands to defend itself? Why didn't it scream? Or run? It lay motionless.

Her headache was back, drumming the scene before her into a watery mist. Why was it here? Why was it even alive?

"Oh, what's the use?" she cried out at last and, setting aside the hammer, wept until a small hand tug-tugging her pantleg brought the kitchen back into view. The knife and hammer on the counter. The crock and tag on the floor. Beside the stove, a teacup that wouldn't ever truly belong to her. Not for all her washing. She looked down.

"I might could have give you the moon," the tiny voice said, "for I don't know what a *Pickled Negro* can do. But you—"

She looked deep into its dark eyes, hoping to see the end of the rainbow and seeing a flat road of tar instead. A road to Everyday and Nowhere.

"—you who pay wit nuttin, get nuttin in return."

The *Pickled Negro* let himself out, leaving the crock and the tag behind,

SPARROW

Juanetta had passed the abandoned house since third grade and paid it no mind. She didn't pass close because now that she was in high school she walked in the street. But one afternoon, when the street was freshly tarred, she was hurrying beside the hedge along the property and without warning pitched forward and vomited.

She ducked into the yard to think. Her sister had a baby at fourteen and it looked like she was following in those footsteps. Mama never said, "None y'all girls worth a damn," but inside her head Juanetta heard those words in her mother's voice.

As she cried on the stoop of the house, hidden from passersby, she noticed a flurry of activity inside the hedge. She had the feeling of being watched. Sure enough, at the end of the yard, a sparrow tilted its head from the branch of a mulberry tree. Slipping sunflower seeds from her bookbag, she scattered them across the hard-packed earth and waited for the sparrow to come down. It hopped, closer . . . closer. Just as she might touch it, it gave a loud cry and a flock rose from the hedge. Snapping like a sheet, it dropped so quickly she lost sight of her sparrow among the dozens. But when the last husk was turned over, the bold sparrow rose first. With a full throat, it led the flock back to the hedge.

When she checked, there wasn't a sparrow to be found, but along the hedge, fresh-hoed earth sprinkled with green shoots. Like beans, she thought. Germinating in a Dixie Cup on the windowsill at school. Alive. In the time it took to retrieve her bag, the shoots had sprung into a row of collard greens, and in a blink of an eye, they were silver with frost.

Perfect. "I can practically smell them cooking down with a turkey wing," thought Juanetta, her mouth watering. But when she tried to pick them, her chest tightened with fear. What had the science teacher said about eating vegetables grown in the city soil? There were bad chemicals in the air and water, lead from the cars. Poison.

She stared at the greens, hungry, unsure what to do, when a long clear cry came from the mulberry tree. Gathering up the greens, she hurried away.

There was nobody home. She cleaned the sink, then rinsed and inspected each leaf like she'd been doing it her whole life. She jumped when the pot buckled with heat and tossed in garlic and onion before the oil burned. Then leaves.

Mama was overcome. "Lord, if I don't smell greens! And how they fresh too?" But then she stirred the pot and frowned. "Why you didn't use the turkey wings?"

Juanetta had no answer for why she changed her mind or how she'd known about the iron skillet. Mama's lip curled. "That old spider gonna leave a rusty taste."

But Juanetta turned the cornbread out on the counter, and it tasted fine. She explained how she wiped the skillet clean with oil and kept it in a hot oven.

Mama fixed herself some of everything. "Who you ever seen do that?"

Again, Juanetta had no answer, and Mama didn't speak more, though she hummed a good deal. Juanetta decided to put off telling her about the other business.

The next afternoon she didn't hear a peep from the hedge. When she checked the other side, the soil was ash-colored and stingy as the rest of the yard. Nothing growing but food wrappers. She rubbed her belly, then sat eating sunflower seeds. Soon she felt eyes watching and there it was. The bold sparrow in the tree. It summoned the flock to Juanetta's scattered seeds, then led them back.

When she checked, there were no birds but once more green shoots growing in dark, loose soil. She blinked and a row of tomato plants appeared, the plum-shaped fruit glistening like someone had only just watered. She weighed one in her hand like a little heart, wondering if it was safe when the sparrow cried out from the mulberry tree as it had the day before. She picked the whole crop and hurried home.

Mama leaned over the sauce, the edges of her hair crinkling from steam. "Did you add sugar?" Juanetta shook her head. "Wouldn't a fatty pork chop be nice?" But nothing was needed, not even hot sauce. "Hungry Mama," thought Juanetta, as her mother mopped the pot with the last piece of cornbread.

All winter, Juanetta fed the sparrow and its flock and found something growing. Even after the snow came, she harvested cucumber, pole beans, corn, celery, and things she didn't have a name for, like romanesco and rutabaga. And every day, when she got home, she prepared supper. As the days multiplied into weeks, there was more food than two bellies could hold. She read cookbooks from the library and by Christmas stocked the freezer and put up preserves.

Mama didn't say so, but Juanetta saw she was glad she didn't work all day to come home and have to cook. Glad Mama. Hungry Mama. Meal after meal, she licked her fingers, sucked her teeth, never mentioning Juanetta's belly. Juanetta thought her secret was safe because now they were both fat.

But we ain't elephants. One spring day, eight months from her first hankering for greens, Juanetta stepped out of the yard with potatoes and a baby.

"Fingerlings," she told Mama. They looked like their name. Chubby child fingers roasted deep brown in the skillet. Skin peeling like wax.

Mama eased into the kitchen chair, smiling at them odd taters dressed with pads of butter and began to eat . . . and eat . . . and eat . . . had popped an itsy-bitsy fingerling in her mouth, was polishing off a smidgen of greens knit to her fork, when there was a whimper from Juanetta's jacket.

"You all right?" Mama said. "Sound like your stomach trying to tell me something."

"Well," says Juanetta, looking for a way to bring up the baby. "You know how I always be bringing home food."

There was a flutter under the jacket.

"You got something else?" says Mama, washing everything down with a glass of cold water. Juanetta wasn't sure whose heart was pounding against her chest. Nothing left to eat, it was now or never. She pulled the tiny thing from her jacket, and Mama leaned forward, smacking her lips.

"You got *that* today?"

"Yes, Mama. I went to dig up potatoes and there it was."

Mama knew Juanetta was lying and decided to teach her a lesson. "Well, what you waiting for?"

Juanetta stood up, scared. "What you mean?"

"I mean split it like a chicken."

Juanetta took a step back.

"Roll it in flour! Fry it up!"

Juanetta clasped the little sparrow to her chest and told the truth.

WHITE FLIGHT

The first day of spring, winter returns like a mother-in-law with too many suitcases. I lay out Mr. Jones's black suit and tell him, "You plan to shovel this snow, you may as well dress for your funeral."

When he don't come back, trapped somewhere inside a glass globe, I guess, I put a ham in the oven and fix pound cake, sweet potato pies, macaroni and cheese, and greens. By nightfall the gang catch a whiff.

PeeWee and Turtle lead the parade, digging a path from the sidewalk to my front door. One flinging to the left, other to the right, their shovelfuls of snow, lifted by the gusting wind, are pretty as white doves. Tiny comes behind with a metal bucket. Wrapped in a scarf so only her eyes show, she casts salt for Brenda, tiptoeing like a bride, her arm tucked under Bird's. Pressed against his other side are record albums. In that arm he cradles a sack of brown liquor as tenderly as he does Brenda.

It's a houseful. Bird taking over the turntable don't bother me because we both Jackie Wilson fans. But you know how you have friends who never met, but you always telling them about each other? You're nervous they won't like each other and don't know what you'll do if they don't.

Smelling like menthol cigarettes, Mr. Hezekiah slips in while everyone's loading up in the kitchen. And it's okay. They tell him how good he looks, considering how long it's been since he lived here, and you can tell he appreciates the compliment.

"Always been a restless soul," he says. "But if I hadn't died when I did, this here storm would have killed me sure."

He lets a conversation between PeeWee and Turtle buzz around his head without swatting. They don't mean any harm and they good-hearted.

"How old he is?"

"He look to be about thirty-five."

"I heard everybody come back is thirty-five."

"What happen if they die before thirty-five?"

"How I know?"

"Why everybody not come back?"

"You sure they don't?"

I want to hear if Mr. Hezekiah has any answers, but there's rustling in the cupboards. Tiny, poking around for a plate and foil, like she always do.

The cold breeze that came in with Mr. Hezekiah ain't hardly heated up when Ricochet, my friend Pearl's boy, rings the bell. He got a new girlfriend, nervous little thing and skinny like she don't eat. Ricochet don't look comfortable either, not with the way PeeWee and Turtle go straight at him.

"Take your jacket, Ricky?"

"Wish your mama could join us."

I tell them hush and welcome Miss Itty-Bitty to my humble abode, then steer her and Ricochet to the kitchen. "I don't eat pork," she says right off the bat, while he digs in. Now Ricochet don't say, "I miss Mama's cooking," but I can see it in the way he's working those flavors through his mouth. It's why he's here.

I stay at the sink alone, thinking, until Brenda ask if I need help. When I say I got it under control, she slide an arm over my shoulders and whisper, "Charlene, every rose has its thorn." It's our private joke. I'm supposed to say, "And every path has its puddle," only the words won't come.

"Just give me a minute," I say instead. "I be my old self directly."

By the time I get back to the living room, setting a piece of pie in front of Mr. Hezekiah, everybody's made themselves comfortable. Same

drunks. Same flirts and fools. Brenda winking at me as her thorn, singing loud and holding a fork for a microphone, tease like *Reet Petite* a girl
he used to be sweet on. PeeWee using the distraction to polish off Bird's
liquor. Turtle pretending to hit on Ricochet's girl, pretending because
it's no secret he prefer plenty of chicken on his bones and he only acting
like Romeo to make Ricochet puff up. Unbothered by the noise, Tiny
is dozing with the TV on mute, her left leg kicking off and on like she's
fighting alongside Bruce Lee. It's what I call the madness after the pro-
digious hilltops of February. Human living. Like maybe the only way
forward is down.

In the brief pause of one album finishing and Bird shuffling through
the others, Mr. Hezikiah rescues Miss Thing from Turtle by saying he
didn't catch her name. She gives it like she don't care to have it in his
mouth, then adds, "And who are you?" like it's killing her.

"Hezekiah," he says, holding onto his lapels. "You looking at the very
first Negro meter man in the city."

That gets everyone's attention, even Tiny opens her eyes a slit, and
Brenda signals Bird to cut the music.

"When was that?" PeeWee ask.

"Back when Mulberry was a white street." He gives me a big grin. "I
know every house on this street, especially this one."

For a second the hairs on my arm rise, like the first time we met by
the washing machine. I gave up trying to make Theodore believe a long
time ago.

"No disrespect," Turtle pipes in. "Mulberry been Black before the
Dawn of Time."

"Even before that," PeeWee adds

"No disrespect taken," Mr. Hezekiah says, with a wink at us ladies.
"But it wasn't always sugar and spicy around here." In those days, white
homeowners sent him ahead of them down the steep basement steps.
With them at his heels, a shove away from serious injury or death, he
kept his hand firm on the banister, wobbly as it might be.

"It pissed me off until I hit on the idea of a fake report."

"What's that he say?" says Turtle, but PeeWee tell him to hush and let the man talk.

"I get to that in a minute," says Mr. Hezekiah. "I looked around at the wet walls and cracks and warned them they was wasting heat as quick as we was pumping it out and being in the middle of an energy crisis, as we were, I was legally bound to report it to someone downtown who would quadruple the bill and add a fine."

"You lied?" says Ricochet's girlfriend. Not as mealymouthed as she looked.

We all hear muffled laughter before Ricochet, a line of sweat over his lip, tugs at his sleeve. He ignores Turtle's second offer to hang it up, and Mr. Hezekiah, being the gentleman he is, treats the interruption like a sincere question.

"Sure, I lied. And got better the more I practiced. It was a wild guess, but I made one man shit his pants by mentioning the city levies a fine for water heaters not installed by a licensed electrician. Found out later it was true."

"Ain't none of them catch on?" Her trembly voice grates. A rule follower like my Theodore. Goody Two-shoes. Rather shovel himself to a heart attack than be fined for not clearing the sidewalk. "Weren't you scared they'd call the head man?"

Mama always set a place for the dead, and Mr. Hezikiah hasn't lost his appetite. He eyeballs Tiny pinching off her foiled plate and picks up the slice I'd set in front of him.

"No nervous Nellies in heaven," he tells her, spilling the beans between bites. "In the here and now, you got to stay ahead of the storm."

"What you mean?"

Except for Ricochet, we laugh into our hands at the nervousness in the girl's voice, wondering if she know he mean her and where she bound to wind up with her sanctimonious self.

"I shine my flashlight into they shitty basements and they turn around and offer me coffee and a donut." He stares around at the four walls of the living room. "In this very house, bribes to get me telling who got the worse house on the street. Digging for dirt." He laughs that big old Sanford, Florida laugh the cold can't kill. "Call the head man? They was looking at him. Afraid of what he knew, who he might tell. And they started clearing those damn steps."

The girl shakes her head like some church mother, and I wonder if she and Ricochet met in bible study. He must be getting desperate. My answer comes quick.

"God don't countenance liars."

The rest of us turn to see Mr. Hezekiah's reaction. He's as cool as a cucumber. As patient as a saint, pausing to thank me for the pie with a long appreciative hum.

"Maybe so," he says at last. "But God who knows it all, knows some days felt like hell. After I retired, work stuck in my head like a bad dream. Couldn't shake it. Then that week of my funeral—"

"—your what?"

A long sucking sound that ain't ham stuck between his teeth means Ricochet about to lose his shit up in my house. He gets the willies at any mention of the dear and not-so-dear departed. A coward.

"As I was saying, the week of my funeral, somebody reported I'd broken in."

"Come on, baby," says Ricochet, putting her into her coat and steering toward the door. "We out of this old folks party."

Mr. Hezekiah jabs his fork after them like a pitchfork and the gang titters.

"Truth is, I wasn't above some good old-fashioned spookin."

Miss Itty-Bitty puts the brakes on her heels and marches back into the room like she gonna set him straight.

"Now you out-and-out lyin," she says all huffy-puffy. A big act because if she was white, she'd be white as a sheet and nowhere near our Mulberry Street.

"Believe what you like, but I was here. White people sold these houses quick because of one spook—and you looking at him."

He pokes the last piece of crust in his mouth, and a glow comes over his face. I know that glow. He thought the pie's deliciousness was the filling when it was the crust all along. My special recipe that nobody living knows. But the mood turns tense as Ricochet throws his shoulders back. At least he got sense enough not to raise his clenched fists.

"You old haint need to stop scaring my girl."

Old? Now why he got to go and say that when some of us old enough to have changed his diaper? Serves him right when he starts slapping his own left leg with his left arm and hopping from foot to foot like the holy ghost got a hold of him. Or a demon. The girl thinks so, making the sign of the cross and squeezing noises out of her teeny voice box, "Devil, leave this man's body."

Mr. Hezekiah shakes his head like you can't fix dumb, and turns his serious feelings toward Ricochet, crying because his left hand is now beating him upside his own head. We all trying not to laugh but PeeWee and Turtle have their hands on their knees, and Brenda's face is buried in Bird's jacket. I think Tiny back in the kitchen, but I don't dare miss a second of the floor show.

"Boy, stop! If you this heated up, why you don't take off that jacket?"

"I will not and you ain't making me . . . baby, we outta here."

But baby's feet ain't moving. "What he talking about?" she squeaks, looking around the room for someone to stop laughing and explain things. She hits Ricochet on the other arm. "You ain't fixin to fight are you?"

"Just tell her!" Bird snorts. "She gonna find out sooner or later."

"Tell me what?"

Ricochet stops slapping and hopping, relieved to do as he's told. Peels off his jacket, then his shirt, and shows her the tattoo of his mother on his left bicep. Only no tattoo that girl ever saw. My Pearl, lipstick as fresh and straight as the day she promised to take my pie recipe to the grave. Her complexion so firm and even-colored it almost makes me jealous. She still the life of the party too. I blush, then bust out laughing when she cuss.

"Go ahead and fuck her, Fool. I'll be right here watching."

Turning this way, that way—if the girl were white, she'd evaporate from sheet to smoke and still not escape Mr. Hezekiah. Wrapping his dark lips around the air like it were a trumpet in Jackie Wilson's band, "Boo!" says he, and she's out the door, Ricochet running to catch up, the gang convulsing in belly-cramping howls. The two of them slip and slide, then vanish into billowing snow.

When did the music start again? Bird rocking Brenda in his arms as the others, glasses refilled, collapse after a good laugh. From across the room Mr. Hezekiah sees how I'm not just tired but crushed, grieving Pearl like her passing was ten minutes ago instead of a year. And for better, for worse, Theodore gone too. He turns, his eyes closed, lip-synching so perfectly you think the song is coming from him and not the turntable.

"Where he gone?" Turtle asks because he can't see him no more. None of us can.

In that split second, my arm prickles, like little needles stitching deep into the skin.

A RARE OLD BIRD

Weekday afternoons. All summer, unless it rained, an old woman sat on the edge of a low pool, soaking her ankles. From time to time she waved a hand toward children attempting to mount the cement Neptune and his spouting courtiers in the middle. "There, there!" she would call out. "Play nice." And the children would settle and the dozen or so mommies chatting on their side of the pool would smirk and the dozen or so nannies on the other would nod without a break in their secretive whispers, while the old woman perched as comfortably as a bird midway between them. Then, close to four, the sun would begin to dip behind the tower of the insurance company, the highest building in the city, and a shadow, straight as a chastening finger, would darken the water. The temperature barely changed but it felt colder and women from both camps pulled sweaters from their bags. "Fifteen more minutes," the old woman would call out, lifting her feet to dry before the sun completely missed the pool. This time all of the women smiled because it is universally good to have someone else to blame for stopping the play.

At 4:15, by the time and temperature sign at the top of the tower, the old woman routinely pulled worn-down flats over her ashy feet, then stood to announce it was time to go. But next the begging would start, cries of "little longer" and choruses of "please-please-please," and crouching to the children's height, she would cup her ear below a clean, bright headscarf.

"What's that?" she asked the worst of the whiners, those with the temerity, she thought the word only to herself, to tug at her best house dress. "What's that? What's that? Well, just five minutes more."

Five minutes more was the signal for the women to gather bags and begin stretching out children's names like they were pulling them in on a clothesline for the night. "Brit-ney!" "Sa-ra!" "Ritch-ie!" "Su-sie!" There are always fewer names than children, so of course there was kindly laughter when the old woman warbled, "Brit-ney!" It had been a popular name for the last five years. A name destined for a fine life no matter how many possessors it happened to have. It was also an unexpected cause of distress at the start of the summer.

"Which one is your Britney? Which girl exactly? What color is she wearing?"

It was rare that lines of communication crossed boundaries, and no one ever spoke to the old woman, so although well within hearing, she paid no mind to the flushed interrogator. When the questions were repeated more loudly, she finally shook her head and looked up. By then every ear around the pool was attuned.

"Green," she said, disguising her embarrassment with a slightly haughty tone. With flocks of children, including several Britneys and flashes of green everywhere, her answer should have been the end of it.

"That one . . . or that one?"

There was an awkward pause during which the old woman squinted in several directions before pointing definitively toward the largest flock. "Yes. That one there."

The woman's eyes narrowed skeptically. "And what agency do you work under?"

Before the old woman could answer, a nanny jumped to her feet and began pointing and shouting strange words at boys playing King of the Mountain on top of Neptune's arms and shoulders. Her cry sent the mommies stampeding toward the source of trouble. When they returned, order restored, the red-faced mommy stared about in confusion before locking eyes on the old woman, relocated several feet away. Not among the nannies, but closer.

Curiosity resurged from time to time, but its rude edges were smoothed by routine into something more natural and unarticulated. A titter. A glance. Each afternoon, at 4:30, the old woman joined the raucous group leaving the park in a long parade of backpacks and plastic baskets brimming with toys, the children whining and hollering, some in tears, others in outright revolt, and the women promising treats and sometimes, in frustration, a good paddling at home. Despite the chaotic rush, the infrequent newcomer might strain her neck to learn which child belonged to the old woman, but in the end the children resisted sorting, were an army close to complete mutiny, a few invariably sprinting in an entirely different direction, usually toward the food vendor at the opposite end of the cement walkway around the park.

"Britney!" Sometimes even the old woman might throw up her hands and holler in frustration, unable to catch hold of her girl from among the indistinguishable little girls flapping and chittering like sparrows. There were mothers in the group who privately cheered her meltdown. For them, it confirmed that the naughtiest were those entrusted to caregivers by working mothers. The nannies, always attuned to this particular shift in thinking, would beam a warning to the old woman that incompetence reflected badly on them, and she would instantly smile and sing out, "There you are, my darling Britney. Wait up! Wait up!" And the mommies, who the moment before had felt superior, were deflated, wondering how, with a full schedule of cooking and bath and bedtime ahead, this flat-footed granny could maintain a positive attitude.

Overall, it was a pleasant, uneventful summer until the sweltering afternoon in August when the heat had wilted everyone's mood. Even the old woman's scarf, always neatly arranged, had migrated above a damp gray hairline as though disavowing her frown. Around half-past three a man appeared. The old woman, stiffening into a defensive posture, watched him weave through the brick entrance, loudly wishing everyone in his path a good afternoon. Ignored by one and all, he began making his way toward the fountain when she rose from her foot bath and shook a finger.

"Stop it right there!"

Then stepping from the water, unconcerned by the scarf escaping to the cement, she waddled towards him, flapping her arms aggressively.

"It was like she had magical power," a mommy whispered to her husband that evening, for the man, his face flushed with drink, instantly plopped on a bench and picked up a discarded newspaper. Despite his rumpled suit and scuffed shoes, he appeared nearly respectable, whereas some of the children were now waving and waddling in imitation of the old woman. One boy was circling her scarf with a stick.

"Our Sara was beside herself with the giggles," the mommy reported with a laugh. "Honestly. I almost peed my pants at how much nigger hair was under that little scarf. And white. Pure white."

But next, as she told it, the fun ended with the old woman fixing her head cloth in a few practiced motions and chiding the children, the boy with the stick nearly to tears, in a tone both gentle and firm. The mommy's eyes scanned the living room carpet strewn with toys and books and her voice turned wistful.

"It was like watching Mary Poppins."

"Aha," said her husband, catching the drift of her thoughts. "A rare old bird. But we can't afford one."

By 4:15 the man was gone, the paper scattered across the grass. And at 4:30, patting a soft head here and there, the old woman, her round face set in its normal, placid expression, brought up the rear of the parade sluggishly winding out of the park. She wrinkled her nose at the garbage cans near the archway where the women tossed half-eaten lunches as they filed past, barely disturbing the little sparrows already picking apart the bread. Cotton sticking to their skin and hair, matted or frizzled, the mommies and nannies looked more like cousins than rivals as they poked and prodded the older children, while keeping a grip on the sticky little ones slung over their shoulders.

Emitting a last call for "Britney" that sounded more like a lament, the old woman struggled to keep up with the leftward turning crowd before seizing hold of a lamppost to catch her breath. But then, with a quick pivot, as though she had forgotten something, she hurried back to the archway. Tucking her head below the metal letters of *Mulberry Park*, bolted in brick, she returned to the birds.

THE FLAT WORLD

When the World was a scattershot of rocks, the upper block of Mulberry Street was a sliver floating in space. Untethered and unbalanced, the upper block held its tenuous position by tending to tilt downward. Sometimes at an angle that defied imagination, and sometimes with deadly consequences.

There were tragic stories of Big Wheels flying over the edge and children tumbling behind a puppy or escaping a pit bull. There were cautionary ones, too. A girl in pigtails, birthday gifts stacked to her eyeballs, chasing down a balloon. A boy, his cheek fat with a wad of gum or Jawbreaker, last seen craning his neck toward the west, coveting the roundest, reddest lollipop at the edge of the World. All of them vanishing into the gaping chasm at the bottom of the block.

It took courage to leap the chasm, but generations of children persisted. They had no choice, for their names were entered into the records. With hearts in their throats, they leapt. Through rain and sleet and snow, they leapt. Through dark of morning, hopscotching to a crumbling rock and withering flag. To pledge allegiance to a world that didn't exist. The indivisible one.

Twice a day. Twelve years. Or less. Or more. And then . . . then what?

If there was one adult to credit for preparing the boys for the final rite of passage—work in most cases, university for a few—it was Mr. Washington, who lived in the house at the very top of the block. After a shift at the plant, when he'd emptied his pockets of change and candy bars for a daughter he claimed to have spit out himself, he hurried outside to throw a football.

Run . . . catch! Run . . . catch! Teetering at times, learning to recover in mid-fall—oh! how the backwards and sideways running boys would run, trusting their mentor to send them to the very edge of the chasm and not a hair over.

"Run, motherfucker, run!" he would shout. Again and again. "Same goddam play!"

At night, one heard him curse much worse at his wife, a kitten of a woman, but this was considered a private matter. The adults, and not just those who attended church, consoled themselves that Mr. Washington, the imperfect servant, was doing God's work: shaping the clay of those He had made in His image.

What happened to the girls? The afterthoughts of creating men? What did they do those afternoons when the boys and Mr. Washington took center stage? What preparation did they make for the future? Like Russian Dolls, each one, save the infants, was in charge of one littler still, this set including treacherous boys who defected as soon as they learned to cross the street. Toddlers, dragging dolls by the hair or pushing trucks, were barely tolerated by girls wobbling side to side on training wheels, themselves suffering the taunts of the artful mid-rangers playing jacks and turning rope. Those on the cusp of womanhood were of extreme camps, connected only by age and disdain for crumb snatchers. The shyest read indoors, inured to infant cries, while the meanest amused themselves by assaulting the make-pretend mommies. Stealing their babies and toppling cups of invisible tea.

The womanish girls, who the old-timers said could smell themselves, hovered above the rest. Nails pressed or painted, edges laid, they staked out a catwalk to show off their pedal pushers and knotted blouses. Hands on hips, they strutted, pivoted, paused, then began again, varying the length of pivots and pauses to shake their heads and with a side-eye simply say, "This here. This street. These damn babies. These worthless boys. It ain't shit."

Mr. Washington kept an eye on them too. Some said, too close an eye, but his brother Melvin, when visiting from back home, wasn't having it.

"Where a man supposed to look? They need to stop shaking they titties in his face."

Irene Washington, twelve and flat and hard as a washboard—her father affectionately called her "Tank"—stayed indoors. Winter or summer, while her mother swept up the broken dishes, put the furniture right side round, and patched her bumps and bruises, Tank stayed in bed, a book propped on her knees, unconcerned by the frustrated nape of hair dampening her pillow and the pimples on her chin, dark and thick as stubble.

clink, clink

She barely glanced at her father filling her piggy bank. More money for candy and books.

clink, clink

Not a thank you or hello.

"Not your fucking business!" he roared whenever her mother pointed this out.

A mortal woman who marries a god is shackled to inertia; the demigods she produces are often vengeful, always capricious. One Saturday night, when she was thirteen, Tank called the police. The actual po-lice for whom the chasm was barely a speed bump.

"He's a drug dealer," she whispered. "I prefer to remain anonymous."

Despite his powers and the paucity of his herb supply and paraphernalia, a single joint in the seat of the car and a rusty scale at the back of the closet with trophies and a high school yearbook, Mr. Washington went away. While it became a quieter, duller summer for the boys, Tank blossomed. She joined the strutting girls and egged on the football players, two of whom went over the edge.

Mr. Washington came out changed. From his spot on the porch, he sneered at the football games proceeding without him and hissed at the children summoned home by wary parents. The sound of his tongue sucking the back of his teeth reduced the little girls to bubbling snot, while the grownish, their stomachs instantly seizing up, passed clots the size of grapes.

One person was unimpressed by the scar that cut his face in half, was unshaken by his tattooed arms. Only one noted how the sight of a police cruiser made his right hand tremble, and how his pecs were not buffed like you see in the prison movies, and understood that behind the bluster, he was broken. Tank.

Her mother still meowed and curled when he spoke, automatically depositing herself for his convenience, but for nearly two years nobody had stopped Tank from going out at night and nobody could stop her now. In his absence, she'd stolen her mother's money to win favor of the neighborhood children, some of whom were not nearly as boring as she imagined, before abandoning them for an older crowd down in the projects. Her new friends said Mulberry Street was nothing but snobs.

Nowadays she wore an oversized T-shirt, so white it hurt your eyes, and a pair of loose fitting jeans draping her hips. Holding up the waistband while thrusting her free arm forward for momentum, she leapt the chasm with the surprising grace of a nanny goat. And when Mr. Washington, rolling back on the balls of his feet, roared, she angled her head as if she bore horns and flared her nostrils.

"You bes leave me and Mama alone."

He knew who to blame. Whose head to mash up to the wall, the better to hear. But he was reduced to muttering, "You turn my daughter against me! You low-down bitch."

An angry man can be sated with someone's flesh under his fists. An angry god needs disaster on a large scale. It was a night when Tank was out. Bone of his bone. His metal heart. When the street was as silent as death, he stepped outside, whistling long and low, "Come out, come out, wherever you be. All you desire on Mulberry Street."

Height, muscles, long hair, light skin, high grades, passing grades, baby dolls, bicycles, candy . . . a spot on the NFL . . . the NBA . . . a record deal . . . fresh sneakers . . . video games . . . latest game system . . .

newest phone—house after house, boys and girls emerged in bed clothes, dreams floating like bubbles over their heads. Big ones and midsized, some swaddling infants in their arms, others toddlers on their hips. Each one, the best hope of a family, tracking the bright egg he lifted over his head and threw a little bit higher than all those months ago, a little bit longer. "Run, motherfuckers, run," he whispered, and they began to race, some backwards, some forward, all of them at once—it happened quickly—until the street disappeared beneath their feet.

At noon, Tank trotted up the block in those jeans Mr. Washington threatened to burn. Nimble as ever, impervious to the severe angle of her ascent and oblivious to cries issuing from every house, she dipped her right hip when she stepped, adding a bounce in sync to Michael Jackson shrieking through her earbuds. Halfway along, she was mobbed by parents pleading to know if she'd seen the others. *The others?* She got the gist of the situation before her mother, fighting the crowd, shouted, "Faith and prayer are real because I've been on my knees since morning."

Above the bowed heads, Tank saw a killer in her father's smirk as surely as she saw the fool in her mother's lie. But it was the gravity of her own part in the tragedy, the loss of the children, that compelled her to break free and gallop back toward the chasm. Though she had grown up fast, she had grown up among them.

To those watching, one arm was too short to reach heaven, so she extended the other, her white shirt testing the air like angel wings. On the verge of flight, her legs became entangled in those blasted jeans, and she sank instead.

SQUATTER'S RIGHTS

FELIX

Born in the aftermath of a hurricane, the son of two childless farmers was lucky. Instead of wailing the loss of a season's crop, Mama fed on his plastered head as though it were a new potato coated in butter and sprinkled in salt. When she licked her lips, finding him perfectly delicious, Papa, his waders muddied to the hips, roared in happiness. Lucky-lucky, the boy receiving the patriarch's full blessing . . . or almost full, for with a sudden lurch from Mama and a howl of pain, a shadow-self (black as a paper silhouette) stained the fresh linen. This fragile hitchhiker, inspected in the soft morning light and given the choked remains of the blessing, was set aside while her brother primed a pump with one fat hand and emptied the other in three greedy gulps.

Lucky, enough, was the second born, postponing a reunion with her sibling on the hill above the house. Lucky enough indeed, and still alive at noon, slipped inside a knitted booty and pinned to her mother's pillow.

"A helper for the kitchen," Papa hinted, for he had missed two meals and wouldn't tolerate a third. Nestled with her babies, in no great hurry, Mama sampled the pilgrim's ear.

"A cull potato," she crooned, "is a potato still."

Luck, as the saying goes, is a Lady. At the start of this story a fickle one, who, like a horrible granny, had a favorite. She indulged the boy. Fed him by hand like a trained bird and multiplied his father's blessings. Felix was never "It" in hide-and-seek and never the one to catch a cold or step on a rusty nail. First to the table, first in his class, first to shout "olly olly oxen free," he was a survivor of wild berries and mushrooms that could kill a grown man.

Luck taught him to flip pennies, earning himself extra lunches and, by sixteen, when he went catting after bedtime, introduced him to dice shooters and card shufflers in the back-alley clubs in town. His stakes began small, then grew to a small fortune which she taught him to bury in the woods. Felicia, the thwarted tagalong, found it out and made a Devil's bargain for the details: the dark liquor and wild music that spun men into a frenzy of dancing and triggered fights over the prettiest partners. She teased him about the women. Leaving off her chores, would roll a cloth in her crotch and perform comical imitations of his attempts at seduction, and he would clutch himself, bent over with bitter laughter. She, with the same jet-black hair woven low over her forehead and eyes like bits of flint, though never cruel, saw in her twin the truth of the old adage: lucky at cards or lucky at love.

Luck has a way of making fools of us all. One morning she snuck Felix through the back door only to abandon him in his own vomit on Felicia's clean floors. The patriarch, saving him in time from a drowning, was apoplectic.

"What women has poisoned my boy?"

Felix, a true fool, later confessed to Felicia that the evening, before turning on rotgut liquor, had been one of the high points of his life. Luck had introduced him to a stranger who told him about other towns much bigger than town. The stranger promised, "With high stakes, come higher winnings."

"What is his name? What does he look like?" Felicia begged to know, but Felix stayed tightlipped.

"A good friend," he said. And sure enough, if friendship can be calculated in dollars and cents, Felix had the best friend a man could imagine. He seemed to have hit the jackpot, but that was Luck's final farewell. Giving him enough rope to hang himself as she found another favorite.

FELICIA

"Why can't you come along?"

Felicia stared from her brother to her stunned parents. Right after Papa announced his decision to move North, Felix announced he was staying put.

"I have a steady job at the mill," he reminded them. He hung his head like a bashful boy. "And I'm planning to ask Rosetta to marry me."

"Rosetta?" Mama wailed. "Why haven't I met her?"

Felicia wasn't falling for the trick. "Make the two of them come," she begged their father. "Five of us earning money is better than four."

Papa ignored her and put a hand on Felix's shoulder. "A man has to make his own way."

Mama said if Felix was staying, she would too and mind her garden and raise her first grandbabies. And Felicia, who exchanged letters with schoolmates who'd made the trek, wasn't keen on snow or snobs. She'd been told cleaning white people's houses was no better there and some-times worse. But saying or thinking anything contrary to Papa was a lost cause. When he said "man," he meant man. Even the fictitious Rosetta was under Felix's thumb.

If Papa was suspicious about the money Felix handed over, he shooed those suspicions away like pigeons trying to roost in the barn. He put money down on a house on the corner of Oak and Mulberry, a fixer-up-per, and got a car to drive him and Mama to the factory while Felicia took the bus. For two years, she saw her future in the old women in hairnets, sitting primly with oversized bags on their laps. Her own bag had a sandwich, a travel book to somewhere finer, and an extra sweater for the ride home. Out the window, every young man striding along the sidewalk was a reminder of Felix. Head up and shoulders straight, head-ing into an adventure she could scarcely imagine beyond her paperbacks.

Then one morning at 3 a.m. he called and the world turned upside down.

The mutilated body of a white man had been found back of some fields and now every Black man in the county was sheltered in place. Afraid the operator was listening in, he whispered that he couldn't leave the house without the feeling of being watched. Yes, the door was bolted, the rifle loaded, but fear pursued him through his dreams. Afraid to sleep, he'd been drinking coffee like water.

Because Papa's righteous anger made him tongue-tied and Mama was weeping like Mary at the foot of the cross, Felicia took the phone. He admitted he'd stopped going to work and said she should expect a letter in the mail.

Dear Sister,

Since we spoke, a dozen of our neighbors were beaten and put in and out of jail. And perhaps you have already heard the youngest son of old man Bryant, that one with the lisp, finally paid the price for all last Saturday night. By then I'd been hunkered down a week with Papa's rifle and faithful Herman. But as the saying goes, Satan never sleeps. While I kept watch, protecting our house and land, praying for our friends and neighbors, something has gotten inside.

Imagine Hitler's army goose-stepping along your spine and understand my terror five nights ago as the Bryant place burned. At dawn, I opened the door to make a dash to the privy and old Herman ran off.

The next morning, I woke bloodied and bruised from a dream of hanging and repeated the Lord's Prayer until I could make no sound.

On the third morning, I woke shivering. On the sheet beside me, where Herman lately cowered, was the impression of a body, the spot cold as ice. Didn't I call on the Lord then? This time drawing the rifle under my chin like a sweetheart.

I found a hair at dawn of the fourth morning, long as my arm and red as a poker. And today, under waning moonlight, the owner curls comfortably as the Cheshire Cat. Have I met this creature at a card table or on a drunken spree? She seems familiar. Or perhaps it's her

familiarity with me that makes it feel so. I have begged her to leave by
the back door, but I fear her return.

I have scarce energy to move and not sure I will be able to write
again. Remember me in your prayers, Felicia, and know that I remain
your loving brother.

P.S. Tell Mama I do my best to tend her garden.

"Hold the faith, Brother," she said to the precious paper, "while I
think of a scheme to save you."

After Felicia posted her reply, the long wait began. Days. Weeks.
There were no more phone calls. No letters. Mama said she would get on
a train and carry him out of there, but Papa, growing thinner and greyer
by the hour, urged prayer and patience. Then a notice arrived from the
post office that a box was waiting to be picked up.

They should have specified how heavy it weighed because Papa had
to come back the next day with a friend's truck. Back home he used a
crowbar to unseal the nailed top, as Mama, fearful that here were his final effects sent by a kindly neighbor, clung to Felicia who stood stoically
as a soldier. Inside, a nicer box was fit snuggly into the first and packed
with straw. That box at least had a hinged clasp.

But instead of keepsakes, Felix was inside. Stretched out in his best
suit, he was his usual red-brown pretty but with his hands clasped over
his chest, as still as a corpse. True to his promise to Mama, he had a sack
of seeds for a pillow, and poked into every available space, sacks of soil
filled with tubers, roots, and bulbs. Had he tried to mail himself like
that desperate slave, Henry Box Brown? Or had a kindly friend fulfilled
a dead man's wish? Mama fell out, Papa, trying to lift her, collapsed, and
after Felix's burial in the same simple box, and before the next full moon,
the two of them passed.

Alone in the house, Felicia thought constantly of her beloved brother
imprisoned underground. As soon as the neighborhood moved on to

other gossip, she bribed the groundskeeper to disinter the coffin and deliver it in the middle of the night. Although his complexion had paled, it still held a flicker of the boy he'd been. After hauling the sacks of seeds and dirt into the yard, she fitted herself beside him, as snug as in the womb. For hours she rubbed his cold hand between her own, unsure if she was dreaming or awake as the coarse strands of his hair, growing thick and fast as kudzu, locked them together.

THE HOUSE

Neighbors, who had secretly laughed at the newcomers renting the haunted house on the corner, then delivered food to the dwindling household, now gossiped about how the rent was being paid. The measly girl they'd pitied and helped feed and comfort after the triple tragedy became an object of curiosity and disdain. Not even six months mourning, she left home every evening, her hair teased into a bouffant around her small face and her clothes expensive and stylish like someone who traveled to the city. It wasn't hard to conclude what kind of work she was doing and why she no longer stood at the bus stop weekday mornings or attended Sunday service.

Where the sacks had landed in the yard, a garden flourished. One so lush and lovely, vegetables and fruits, flowers and berries for every season, that their envy was further piqued. The assault began with pulling out the roots, trampling the dirt, pouring bleach into the soil. When invisible actors tossed trash into the yard and broke every window, the most fervent churchgoers, the turn the other cheek crowd, didn't say peep. It appeared nothing less than seeing the girl thrown out the door by the mortgage lender would satisfy the neighborhood, the rival of any crowd at the Coliseum.

Then late one night, the screech of a train went on for hours, shaking the foundations of their houses, after which came pounding, each blow more hellish and powerful than the one before. Not a soul stepped outside until dawn when the crowd jockeyed for a glimpse from the opposite sidewalk. On tiptoes and set upon each other's shoulders, some with ladders, some making futile jumps into the air—none able to see over the thick hedge that now fortified both the house and garden.

SPARROW

"What you got there?"

She didn't mean to frighten the little girl, but she was curious. Unseen in her dark clothes, she had been studying the street. Waiting for that magical hour that comes to every neighborhood when twilight pauses human movement. Her attention had been focused on a crow picking apart a flattened squirrel, when she'd spotted a figure, too large for a dog and holding a shiny object. Whatever it was scurried along the sidewalk before darting into a narrow break in the hedges. Her hands poised to break a neck if threatened, she stealthily followed.

The child was picking eggplants and stacking them in the bowl with the skill of a greengrocer. All the more astonishing because it was barely spring in the North. Another surprise: Confronted in the darkness falling around them, the girl's round eyes, innocent in another face, did not indicate fear but only wariness as they met her gaze straight on.

"I don't talk to strangers."

Such nerve. "No? But you'll sit in their yard and steal their vegetables?"

The girl hissed like a cat. "This is *my* yard and *my* garden. Mama says so."

"Hmph! I have news for your Mama. This is my yard and my garden." She pointed over the child's head. "And that is my house."

The girl jumped to her feet. She couldn't be more than five or six. Wearing a homemade cotton dress with a smocked bodice that emphasized her flat chest which she stuck out like a big woman. Or a bird. Felicia barely suppressed a laugh, and the enraged trespasser put up her fists.

"If it's your house, why you don't take care of it?"

Those words may well have been an arrow to Felicia's heart, for suddenly their roles were reversed. The girl the owner and she the intruder.

37

Even in the dim illumination of the streetlights one could see the peeling gray paint, the spotty shingles on the roof, and the outline of a forest growing in the gutters. She knew it was not simply fall, but with her long absence, a fall. The magnificent hedge was reduced to a hollow globe of bare twig. The eggplants, though purple as the evening sky, were mere tokens of the full splendor of Mama's old garden. Mama and Papa. She had meant to do right by them but frustrated by an absence of luck had made her own and traveled the world. The child, perhaps sensing vulnerability in her distracted thoughts, attacked.

"It's my house because I love it. And today's my birthday and I wished for Mama to make something special and these, whatever-they-are, are special."

Stifling a laugh, she stepped back into the shadows. She wished the child could see how well the inside was preserved, the floors polished and the furniture covered with sheets to keep off the dust. She had known this girl a quarter hour and wanted to show her the collection of lovely paintings on the wall and the magnificent sculptures from renowned artists, some of them friends. She would light the fireplace in the living room and wrap the two of them in warm blankets and tell her stories late, late into the night. Stories that belonged to children but were kept from them by their stupid elders. How pleasant an evening it could be in place of the awkward reunion waiting inside. A lecture, certainly, with words like "duty" and "responsibility" and "loyalty" summoning the spirit of Papa, spoiling the way she'd made out of no way.

She decided to try again with the child. To be nice.

"My name's Felicia. What's yours?"

The girl wiped her nose with her forearm. A tentative softening. "Sparrow."

"Well, Sparrow, those are eggplants. Now how do you suppose something so dark and beautiful grows here with no warm summer sun?"

The girl looked at her as though she'd fallen from a turnip truck. "Mama says it's magic and the best thing to say is thanks."

Felicia was stunned by the naturalness of the answer, for it had taken her years to believe in magic and magical beings, then more years to trust them. To trust herself. In the past months, preparing this return, a finale to cut the final cord and bury the past, she had fought a resurgence of doubt. That this child could spout gratitude for a place that pulled her from whatever corner of the world she hid, made her question those intentions again. Even as a possibility formed in her mind, it was humbling. She knelt before the little sage, careful to keep a distance.

"Well, Sparrow, you appear to have squatter's rights."

"What does that mean?" Felicia saw her balled fists making dirt stains on the light-colored dress, and her decision was final. A child who didn't fear her mother's rage feared no one.

"It means I'm willing to make a deal . . . to give you something."

"I'm not supposed to take things from strangers."

"Ah. But you and I are friends now, aren't we?"

Silence.

"Do you remember my name, Sparrow?"

"Felicia . . . like a girl in my class."

"Yes, yes. You see there are lots of Felicias and we're all very happy and nice."

"I don't like her."

The little devil! "Always an exception. But hey there! I like you and I've decided to give you something of mine."

Sparrow! Sparrow! At the sound of her name called from up the street, the girl's head twisted obediently. A trace of innocence that touched Felicia's heart and fortified her resolve.

"Sparrow? Are you listening?"

Perhaps it wasn't fair that when the child turned back, she wore the expression of someone listening to a cobra. Is that what Felicia had become? She spoke quickly before she hated herself.

"You meet me here on your twenty-first birthday. You understand? I'll give you the key."

"What key? What do I need a key for?"

Felicia stood up and brushed the travel dust from her skirt. "The house, of course." And before the wide-eyed child could ask a question from the dozens doubtless tumbling through her head, Felicia let herself in by the side door.

GRACIE BROWN

In summertime the hill at the southern end of the park was a fountain of green spilling from the massive red water tower at its peak. While half the neighborhood splashed in the public pool near the entrance to the park, the steep lawn overlooking the city was perfect for a Sunday picnic. Unless you asked Gracie Brown, who habitually wore a scarf to keep the wind out of her hair.

"It's not quite perfect," she liked to tell Jackie. "But it's just fine."

In the shade of a spreading oak, she unloaded the basket onto a cotton sheet while he called out landmarks as though newly built over the previous six days. The twin water tower at the other end of the city, the spire of Blessed Sacrament, even the flat roofs and high towers of the university where he worked in maintenance but lauded on Sundays like a treasured alum. There was nothing prettier out there than the lake, a slip of blue fringing the horizon.

"Mr. Brown got me tired out from fishin." Gracie sighed the words so often into the phone her girlfriends pitied her. But there was Jackie, shaking his head in mock disapproval, for while they did get to the lake often, *fishin* was code wrapped up in the lie to get out of Bid Whist and drinks.

Gracie Brown, a drop of perspiration pooling like milk in the dark cave of her collar bone, fixed the strap slipping off her shoulder. She was quick and used her pitching hand to slap him away from the chicken. The same hand that slowly traced his bare chest Saturday night after "fishin." The rebuke was the same too. "Slow down, Mr. Brown. You act like somethin chasin you."

The accusation gave him a chill because, although he kept pace ahead of it, something *was* chasing him. And while life was good, knock on wood, he suspected it was playing the long game, waiting to tell him no matter how hard he hustled, he would gain no ground and lose some to boot. A decade earlier, the year before he met Gracie at twenty-five, the prediction seemed true for he was making payments on what was already breaking down, and finding himself, month after month, more in arrears. He was failing at love too, his lack of money extending to a lack of finesse.

Then one morning he tripped getting off the bus and a woman caught hold of him easy as catching a baseball. And she didn't let go. When she asked where he was off to in such a hurry, meant as a gentle joke in case he was embarrassed, he honestly couldn't remember.

Gracie made it easy to forget. Those early days were filled with the distractions of ordinary worry, silly ruminations which any person newly in love will face. Worry woke him at night, for she talked in her sleep and snored like a man and did indeed play baseball with the Mulberry Sparrows, which meant early rising on Saturdays to use the field before the men. "Like she ain't dark enough," Worry whispered when he cheered with the few husbands and boyfriends in the hot stands. And during those long stretches of nothing between a fast pitch or some field action, when his belly was growling, Worry sneered, "What kind of woman ain't got the sweetness to look over here and wave?"

Worry had ten fingers to count on and ten toes and didn't like that Gracie wasn't but nineteen and after celebrating (mostly) and packing up her gear, she went eagerly to the farmer's market. On top of which, she knew how to fry okra better than any woman who wasn't his mother and scale a fish and clean it. Things he never learned. And everything she did, including the windup to that fast pitch over the plate, she did real, real slow and careful. Was it too slow? Worry thought so. "Pretty soon you be slow right up with her," it whispered. "And poorer than ever."

But a person can change, if they allow themselves to, and see that slow moving can be a virtue, a talent, whose benefits bless both partners. Sure enough, Jackie learned to set aside his own ineptitude at sports and admire her intensity on the mound, the subtle ways she set the tone and pace of the game like an orchestra conductor. It took longer to stop resenting how she rolled the knives and forks in napkins and tied them with ribbon in impossible knots. But because Gracie wasn't going to change and because of those blessed benefits, *he* changed. Without breaking the ribbon or using his pocketknife, he unworked the knot with the same patience it took to watch her wipe off the china plates and jelly jars without saying, "They already clean, Gracie."

But while love survived, fighting Worry with one kiss, one meal at a time, ever so often something flashed in Jackie's rearview mirror. It was hard as a hickory nut and persistent as a coonhound, and cold and metallic, it lodged like a bullet, a fraction of an inch from his heart. He knew he ought to tell Gracie, the problem solver, but the thought nagged him: removing a bullet can be worse than letting it stay.

Saturdays in summer started early and went into the wee hours, but with Gracie managing time, he woke late and refreshed on Sunday morning. Short as summer was, with the chance of rain when you least wanted it, or the unavoidable visit from out-of-towners, she taught him how to stretch the pleasure of an afternoon that was never guaranteed. Whatever they were doing, sitting up to eat, shielded by their tree as the sun hung suspended overhead, or rooting for a kid with a newspaper kite, she made the moment last. The wind moving the grass, the sunlight making each blade part of a cresting wave, a bird wheeling like a kind of kite, a kite stumbling and crashing until, as if guided by Gracie's loud encouragement, lifting gloriously into a blue that rivaled the lake. Whatever small thing was happening around them, Gracie would hold the moment like a ladybug on the tip of her finger and allow him to see its magnificence.

It was always windy on the hill, too windy for Gracie's hairdo, and even a light wind would bother the cotton sheet. At the beginning of the season, a corner flipped into the banana pudding, causing great worry before she saw another way to make the afternoon feel like forever.

"You gonna stand there looking hungry or find me some rocks?"

The first time was easy because there was a copse of oak and maple behind the tower, a place popular for midnight trysts, where the groundskeepers tossed unwanted rocks. The only thing he disliked was dirtying his hands. The following week she repeated the request, but on the next one he produced stakes. Instead of a chaste kiss for his ingenuity, she frowned and avoided watching him. He was compliant the next time, but stashed four small boulders at the base of the tower under its fake portal. The only one who saw through the tall weeds was the carved face of Neptune, admiring the same view of the lake as him and Gracie. But then it rained the following weekend, so by the next one, the mowers had come through, either throwing the rocks with their blades or moving them.

"Wind's picking up, Mr. Brown," Gracie said when he returned empty-handed. He could have sworn she had a laugh tucked up in her smile. This time she pointed him toward the tree line, and he grudgingly obeyed.

It only rained during weekdays in July, sunshine saved up like pennies for Gracie and Jackie's Sundays in the park, but rain and high humidity had turned the undergrowth into a jungle. Unable to see light through the brush, the intense silence making his ears drum, he ran out in a panic, fortunately unseen. Gracie was watching two kites dive dangerously close as their handlers pulled farther and farther apart. When the bigger one flew higher, trailing a tail of brilliant yellow scraps, Gracie danced as if she were a girl, the hem of her dress riding up around her knees.

Feeling put out to be so quickly forgotten and excluded from the fun, as he sometimes felt at the ballpark, he trudged into the woods. And again and again, through August, finding rocks for Gracie so they might eat lunch without the meddling wind.

After Labor Day, when the pool was closed, but summer seemed set on being eternal, the wind picking up without cooling anyone, they continued to picnic. Through his weekly quest for rocks, Jackie had tamped down safe pathways through the forest and, having depleted his reliable sources, branched off to make elaborate connecting routes through the undergrowth. The job was increasingly time consuming, but no matter, he began to tell himself, for at the end of his labors he always found her. Sometimes arranging the bowls and basket as temporary weights in the corners of the cotton sheet, sometimes dancing among the swelling fleet of kites. Always, he decided, testing his faith.

Was it then? During that long string of sunny days that lasted into October? He couldn't remember when he first went beyond the forest. Entered the city again, casing the adjacent neighborhood for a stone wall, a rock garden, a rock path. He was a thief for his Gracie, but he didn't press his luck and returned to where he knew best. Mulberry Street. He was hot, beaten by the long walk and digging rocks from his own back yard. Meaning to have a drink and cool shower before returning to Gracie, he fell asleep.

What time was it? He could hear rain falling on the roof, then the tick of ice, the muffled softness of snow, more rain, then silence. Such dreams. Walking out the back door, he found himself back where he'd started. On the living room couch. He tried the front door, the side; he tried walking backwards, sideways, eyes closed, open, fluttering so that whatever door it was looked like a stack of cards being shuffled. He kept choosing the wrong card, for each time he was farther back from where he thought he had started. Washing his hands at the sink. Removing his shoes at the back door mat. Leaning the shovel against the house. Piling rocks.

Finally. Resting a moment on a metal chair. He couldn't get farther back than there. He shook his head. It was afternoon. No sign of rain or ice or snow. He hurried around the house, stepping into fresh dog shit as the culprit and its guilty owner scurried a half block away. He wiped the soles of his shoes on the grass, relieved he could smell, for he had once read that the sense of smell is absent in sleep.

Finally. Waking with his head crooked in a clearing matted down as smooth as if a deer family had recently bedded. A fern was pressed so hard into his cheek that he could feel the lacy pattern on his skin. A witch. A witch had caught him napping and ridden him while he slept. Ridden him to Mulberry Street and back.

"Took you long enough," Gracie teased. "I was ready to call the FBI."

"Got a little turned around," he said. He tried not to put too much meaning into his next words, a just in case. "Do you know if the new neighbors went and got themselves a dog?"

Gracie handed him a glass of ice-cold tea, the condensation sticking to his fingers. She watched him drink it in one long gulp, then laughed, "You still thinking of that old hunter of yours? Why you don't get another one, Jackie? A dog always find its way."

She was wrong about that, the only thing she was ever wrong about, because he had repeated a lie and not the shameful truth of how he lost Buss Ward when he was five. Stolen out of his father's car and nobody in his family could get him back. That's the way it was down south in those days. Gracie, born and raised in the shadow of this water tower, couldn't be expected to understand.

"Damn dog tore up my back seat," Daddy had griped, like it was the dog's fault somebody with dirty hands had rubbed up against the window, teasing him to distraction before stealing him outright. It took being a man himself to understand his father's misplaced anger.

"It's a beautiful day, Gracie," he whined. "Why we don't just enjoy it?" He pinched her bottom playfully as he spoke, but inside the bullet slipped closer to his heart. By reminding him of Buss Ward, she had conjured something dangerous.

By the next week, the last Sunday of October, the extended summer was in a battle of survival and fall was in the wind. There was a worry on Jackie, toting the picnic basket as Gracie ran ahead. By the time he caught up, she was chattering among a gaggle of kite flyers who had beaten them to the summit. All week, he'd tried to focus on a perfect day, willing the sun to shine even if they needed jackets, praying for the rain to hold off. Well, the weather at least had cooperated. But once the conjuring began, he couldn't stop it. What had happened the previous Friday was always bound to happen.

He was alone on the top floor of the Hall of Letters, finishing up the tall eastward facing window with a squeegee. He liked the hour before the students and faculty arrived, shedding dust and spilling coffee cups, ignoring him like he was one of the orange cones. From the other side of the empty building, he heard the echo of his coworker's keys, a signal to meet outside for a smoke. The window gleaming, he went to use the restroom.

It couldn't have been more than a couple minutes before he came out and found two handprints on the glass. Containing his irritation, he listened for footsteps hurrying downstairs and muffled laughter, but it was silent, and down below, he could see Travis leaning against a wall, his head encircled in ghostly smoke. Angry now, Jackie poked his head into the empty classrooms and checked the stalls. Returning to the window for a clue, he stood before the glass, imitating where the trespasser had stood, gauging the sameness of their height and the size of their hands. This time he noticed a round print where a nose had pressed against the glass, and when he set his eyes in the same direction, his mouth filled with the taste of metal. Miles away, but small enough to set on his finger-tips, the water tower blazed red from the rising sun behind it.

Now as Gracie unpacked the basket, he didn't take his eye off the spired wings of the Hall of Letters, conscious of something watching. The same gust that crashed a little polka-dotted kite back to the ground and car-

47

ried along its tiny owner's wail lifted the sheet, and he felt the something's attention shift to Gracie buttoning her sweater to the top. He wanted the thing as far from her as possible and had a plan, if he could see it through.

"Where my rocks, Jackie?"

She barely caught her scarf as it was pulled from her head, flapping like a flag before she could gather it together. He used the distraction to break off a piece of corn bread for the pleasure of having his hands slapped.

"You gonna wait for me?"

"Like I gotta somewhere else to be!" she laughed. "Beautiful day. Shame to hurry."

He surprised her with a kiss on the lips, then before she could protest, pretended to dart into the woods. As he watched, hidden behind an oak only beginning to change color, she stepped from the shade, rubbing the sleeves of her sweater to warm up, before she went to pick up the much-abused kite that had crashed only a few feet away. After an extended conversation with the child, she held the poor thing aloft and walked it backwards, repeating the action several times as the little girl ran in the opposite direction. At last, by switching positions, Gracie was able to get it airborne and passed it off. Like mother and daughter, Jackie thought wistfully, watching them stare at the silly looking thing and its ragtag tail below the much bigger kites.

Feeling the hackles rise on his neck, he quickly refocused on his plan. There was no time to feel sorry for his exclusion, for something, his rival in size and height, and with the advantage of invisibility, and perhaps speed as well, was close and was closing in. But Jackie knew every inch of the copse, had, by turning over each rock and log and following the deer paths and napping in their beds, stomped a veritable maze through the undergrowth.

The night before he had reflected on his father's decision to move North, surrendering to something that outfoxed them at every turn.

Listening to Gracie's slow even breaths, her long, precious body spooned into his, he understood how there had been no other choice. But there were consequences.

The relief of hearing Daddy, who had gone ahead, laugh from the safety of his aunt's place was one thing, and his sister Nell's fury another. Never missing an opportunity to torture him, she blamed Buss Ward for not fighting his kidnapper like a normal-acting dog.

"I'm leaving Grandpa and my friends on account of a mangy coward," she hissed out of Mama's earshot. "I hate you Jackie Wilson Brown. I'll hate you to my dying day."

Because of Nell he had worried, for a long time, that his father was a coward. He didn't dare say so as a boy, but nibbled around the corners of this thought like it was the crust of jelly bread. By the time he got down to the last little crumb, they were reunited in a cramped city apartment. He asked Daddy a trick question to get at the truth, man-to-man.

"Was it a ghost took Buss Ward, Daddy?"

"Jackie, you know there ain't no such thing."

"Then who don it?"

"We a long way from there, Jackie. It don't make no more difference."

Well, it didn't, but not in the way his father had meant with his disappointing answer. Soon the rumblings of something began again, confirmed by Nell, peeking through a new keyhole, listening with her ear against the wall of a new bedroom. Something had followed them north, then followed them from the projects to Mulberry Street. From what Nell reported from the late-night cursing, it would follow them to the ends of the earth. Which is why Jackie had finally forgiven his father.

His back flush against the stalwart oak, he smelled something pissy in the air, and recognizing his own nervous sweat mixed up in it, resolved to hold his ground as long as possible. He would act nonchalant as a dog panting on the back seat of a car, and when the thing thought it had him, run hard, making a switchback over and over until he had it cornered. Then these hands, wrinkled and gray like an old man's from washing and rewashing the same windows and floors, but strong from constant wringing, would find the neck of the thing, if it had one, and squeeze out its last breath.

Higher and higher the kites rose like a flock, Gracie's long limbs a blur among the flapping children. Between the shrieks of victory and good-bye, he heard her song, *Beautiful day. Shame to hurry.* When it was time, he wiped his eyes, and turning, strolled purposefully into the woods.

A WALK DOWN MULBERRY STREET

REPAST

After the repast crowd left to sleep off her husband's liquor cabinet, the widow heard what she thought was a mouse, scritch-scratching in the cellar. Then there were two, then a dozen, then hundreds, racing from floor to wall and across the beams. As she fled outside, her nightgown hiked above her knees, the house gave a lurch, then lifted on black feet from its foundation.

By the light of the flickering streetlamp, she admired how the feet shifted to the right, now to the left, in order to balance the weight of the house. She cheered the sturdy, calloused heels, capable of long, hard distances, and marveled at the thick ropes of muscle up top, attached like reins to the knotted bridle of each bulb-shaped toe. Ashy, unashamed mud mashers. Feets-do-your-stuff feet. Feets don't fail me now. The very feet she always dreamed of having in place of the soft paws she scampered on.

Not to be left behind, she climbed the basement steps dangling like a rescue ladder between them, so was safely inside when they edged around the mulberry tree, stepped over the curb, and began to lumber down the street emptied by a surfeit of grief.

Because of the slumping porch, jacked up by cinder blocks left behind like slippers, the house was a swaybacked old woman, creaking and complaining with every step. But the feet were resolute. There was such a thunderous rocking and toppling of things not nailed down that the widow, despite her headscarf, sturdy as a tricorn hat, surrendered to the bathtub until dawn's early light when she surveyed the new landscape.

Its backside to the street, the house had settled on the vacant lot at the bottom of the block. In place of a lovely tree, the front door now opened to the chasm that stole the children of Mulberry Street.

RITUAL

Mrs. Washington tended her shrine. Every night before supper, she dusted the school photo, the rattle, the report card, and the overdue library book. Next, she placed a candle among them, watching the flame flicker while she ate her supper on the couch. Then late-late, she got a sweater from a hook in the closet and moved to the porch steps. For hours she searched for a sign from the black, voiceless void that lay at her feet.

There were bereft parents up and down Mulberry Street. Some held steady to their stoop, eyes fixed on the pot of space and the wet paint of the stars. Praying. Others, whom she had known her whole life, believed the children needed coaxing. In the dark, indifferent to Mrs. Washington at her observation post, these mothers and fathers lowered candy by colorful threads into the chasm as if the lost children were swimming about like fish. Whenever a new crack appeared on the sidewalk or street, candy would be left there too. A trail of candy to guide them home. Mrs. Washington saw everything and said nothing about the raccoon who gave the parents false hope.

There was one woman who never came outside. Accompanied by an old man she didn't recognize, the woman's husband stopped by Mrs. Washington's stoop on his way gone and confessed that his wife stayed in the attic where their sons had had a playroom. Eventually she begged him to saw holes in the roof in case the boys returned by comet and, half believing, he had indulged her. Now there was an infestation of squirrels that sounded like a constant birthday party.

"But it has to end. Doesn't it have to end?" he asked Mrs. Washington. "How many times can a heart break?"

"Come along with us," the old man told her with a tap-tap of his cane against the pavement. The sound reverberated inside her hollow chest. "Hope is around the next corner."

She almost asked him to repeat himself, so sweet did his odd words sound, but after a pause waved the two along. She had survived a false god and the loss of her only child. Without her rituals, she would be nothing.

Everyone had a ritual. Leaving pie to cool on the window ledge, keeping the Christmas tree up permanently, fixing a plate before an empty chair. And always, always, when the wind blew down the street close to suppertime, it was perfumed with hummingbird cake and fried chicken. That was a signal for the saddest ritual of all. The roll call. The calling of names to supper.

Mrs. Washington didn't fix a plate and call Irene. No, she did not. Nor do any of those other crazy things. She stuck to her private, dignified business of dusting the shrine before supper and sitting on the stoop until bedtime.

They called her "the widow" because there is no word in English for a mother who loses a child. *Widow,* meant respectfully, for while most women still had a lover or husband to support them, Mrs. Washington lost a husband soon after the children disappeared.

She would have cursed them if she'd known. And they would have tossed her in the chasm if she'd explained why. There was a riddle in her head, you see. A riddle that was part of her sitting on the stoop watching the chasm while the candle burned inside. If she had never met a god named Mr. Washington, he couldn't have done what he did with the children. Which wasn't entirely clear, except that they were gone and he had done something. But if she hadn't met a god named Mr. Washington, she wouldn't have had Irene.

RENEWAL

More years pass. More Christmases and birthdays. More Thanksgivings. More pies. More candy. Same riddle. Over time, Mrs. Washington has eased the strict adherence to ritual. She allows the round cheeks in the metal frame a bit of what she thinks of as powder and appreciates that a spider has knit the rattle to the spine of the book. She approves the lacy stains of misplaced cups that cover grades in gym class and science. The A in English remains. The A in math. Her girl was smart and gifted.

Because of a near disaster, the candle is gone. It was replaced by a candy jar after her neighbor, who must be nearly a hundred, delivered a plump brown baby. A handsome boy with a sweet tooth who has recently learned to throw *Ma-Ma, Da-Da* like little knives into Mrs. Washington's heart. He's not the only one. From her supper table, she hears through the walls of the houses. The children are returning.

There are enough for a school bus. A Sesame Street of simple shapes fills half the windows. Some round, some long and narrow, some square, some triangular. And tonight is Halloween.

She uses a mirror to check between her legs and sees that the hair is sparse and gray. Then well before dusk, she leaves the candy jar open on the stoop. Instead of sitting outside to guess which beloved boy or girl is under the mask, instead of waiting for Irene, who had a round head as a baby but in the photo on the shelf shoulders a misshapen block of tragedy, she climbs the dark stairs of her house. She lingers a moment to consider the door to the attic, then goes to bed.

PATTY-CAKE AND THE TALKING BELLY

"Hey, sugar. Blow on these dice for me."

Patsy had been hearing that, or something like it, her whole life.

"Got a number, baby?"

"Slap Daddy's card."

There was the other stuff. Like knowing Aunt Rose was having a baby and Mama's hooped earring was under the couch. Serious stuff too. "Phone's funny," her belly might say as she was playing double Dutch. She'd stop jumping or turning and go inside to tell. Mama never said, "Leave me alone while I'm talking," like Daddy did. She knew to hang up fast. Then she'd put her soft hand on Patsy's round belly.

"Here. Right here, Patty-Cake. You keep listening to that."

One day she was dancing her teddy bear across the windowsill when she saw a car across the street and a white man hunched low behind the wheel. Her belly said, "Tell Mama," and Mama peeked through the blinds and told her she was a smart little girl.

Daddy was proud too. But he didn't believe in bellies talking, except to say they were hungry or ate too many beans. He called hitting the number and card slapping lucky guesses. "Number gotta come out sooner or later."

"This is a whole new different," Mama said after he came in from staring the white man and his car off the street. "Admit it. Our girl's belly is looking after us."

"Belly, ear, eye, left foot—whatever's doing the talking, there's nothing magical about distrusting white people." He pointed a finger at Patsy's belly, and the scared thing curled up against her backbone. It was six, like Patsy, but she cradled it like a baby doll and hoped it didn't cry.

"That's enough, Chuck," Mama said.

"And that goes for the meterman, the postman, and twice for the census taker."

"I said—"

"Hell! She'd be better off putting her ear to the ground!"

Daddy hooted when Patsy did just that and only stopped laughing because she was crying.

"Something ain't right," her belly whispered, afraid of being yelled at again.

"Something ain't right," Patsy sobbed, afraid of being yelled at too. The linoleum was buzzing like a five-alarm fire.

With Mama behind them, mad and fussing, Daddy took her downstairs to prove the noise was coming from the furnace. It conked out a couple days later.

"Told you so," Mama said. "You owe somebody an apology."

"That belly got a number for me?" he shot back.

"123," Patsy said off the top of her head and Daddy played it for two weeks.

"Threw away good money," he told her in front of a neighbor.

When that same neighbor hit straight the third week and tipped Patsy a dollar, Daddy still blamed belly talk.

"Any number bound to come out sometime."

Mama stayed quiet.

One evening, a month on, Patsy listened to them take turns in the bathroom as they got ready to go out. There was always steady singing from the shower and a long *psssss* before the scent of coconut drifted through the house. No arguing or fussing, but Patsy didn't like it. Their weekly meeting places moved around, and tonight's was in walking distance. They planned a detour to drop her at Aunt Sue's house on Mulberry Street. She didn't like Aunt Sue's furniture with the crunchy covers and the way Aunt Sue ended every sentence with, "Don't make me have to tell you twice." She didn't like Aunt Sue.

The only thing good was her cousin Cap, but he was nearly a grownup and usually off playing baseball in the park. That left her with twelve-year-old Willie. The last time they were alone together, when he was supposed to be showing her his comic book collection, her belly said, "Tell Mama." Except when they came to get her, Mama gave him a big hug and a five-dollar bill for babysitting.

Her belly didn't talk for two weeks.

Daddy came out of the bathroom. His Afro was picked out and sprayed as round and bright as the moon. He was the most handsome man in the world, but tonight she couldn't stop staring at his yellow dashiki. She had a sour taste in her mouth.

"Don't go, Daddy. Please don't go."

The week before she had said the same thing, and they'd stayed home to watch the Ed Sullivan Show. Patsy bunked close to him on the couch, kicking her legs and spilling Jiffy Pop everywhere. When a tap dancer came on the screen, she ran and got her new shoes.

Mama stepped out of the bedroom in a pretty blouse and wide-legged pants. Her Afro was a smaller version of his and looked real nice with the gold hooped earrings that were big enough to fit Patsy's wrist. She leaned up against Daddy, inhaling him like a pot of delicious.

"What's this child hollering about?"

Patsy knew better than to grab around her mother's pantleg, but she wanted to. Wanted to hold on tight and not let go. "Please stay home." Mama's smile melted.

"You created this mess," Daddy said. "How we supposed to get things done with her crying crocodile tears every week?"

She nearly jumped out of her skin when Mama patted her belly like a drum.

"What's the matter, baby? Your belly got something to say?"

Patsy stared down at her patent leather shoes and the little scuff mark from being stepped on at school. *How they feel?* She had known they were perfect, but like that mean girl in class, Mama stole some of the shine by asking the same question over and over. "Don't say they perfect because they pretty. *How they feel?*"

Mama was doing the same thing with belly talk. The more she asked, the less sure Patsy was.

"Tell the truth, Patty-Cake. What your belly say?"

"It say stay home.'"

"You sure?"

"Uhu."

Daddy sucked his teeth, and Mama got in his face. "How you know? How you know nothing happened last week because we *didn't* go."

He picked up the keys, but she was already taking off her earrings, putting them on the coffee table for Patsy to mess with.

"I'm tired anyhow, but be careful, Chuck. Extra careful."

Mama seemed okay while she was popping popcorn and filling glasses of orange soda. Then, just when they were settled on the couch, she jumped up.

"Stay here."

"Mama?"

"Imma run around the corner to check your father's alright."

Patsy shook so bad, she spilled soda on her clean pajamas. She'd never been left alone at night.

"What's wrong, baby? I'll be back in ten minutes."

"Please don't go, Mama."

"You want me to call Willie to stay with you?"

"No!"

Mama's left eyebrow shot up. "Then what you want?"

" My belly say I'm not supposed to be alone and we should eat popcorn and watch TV."

It was a long speech for a belly and sounded a lot like something Patsy would say. Mama frowned. "Was your daddy right? Are them crocodile tears?" She didn't give Patsy a chance to answer. "When I get back, your behind better be in bed."

The next time Patsy saw her parents they were side by side in coffins at the front of the 6th Street Tabernacle Church of God in Christ. They wore matching white daishikis and their Afros gleamed same as the halos of Mary and Jesus in the church windows. Because their eyes were closed, they couldn't see Cap pulling Aunt Sue back to the pew or the way Patsy, a bangle tight around each wrist, kept scooching away from Willie.

NEGRO GIRL'S RITUAL
FOR A MIRACULOUS CURE

"That stank, Miss Ivy."

Miss Ivy winced at the five-year-old plugging her nose at the other end of the couch. She had sprayed, but there was no fooling this one.

"I know, honey," she said. "But it make me feel better."

LeDawn looked sad. "You gonna die?"

"Now who say that?"

"Calvin told my daddy and he say he have no place to live."

Miss Ivy sucked the back of her teeth. "He say anything else?"

LeDawn put her head down. "He say for me to stop dancin."

Miss Ivy didn't let on she'd seen the nasty gyrations through the window, that being the reason she'd called her inside.

"Now look at your shirt. Why you was laying up on the dirty sidewalk?"

LeDawn's eyes got big. "I was listening to the crack, Miss Ivy."

"Crack? What you doing that for?"

"The lady."

"What lady?"

"The one who say, 'Dance, LeDawn. Shake what your Mama gave you and can't take back. Stomp your feet.'"

Miss Ivy's chest tightened with worry. "Who this lady? Where she at?"

"In the crack, Miss Ivy. The lady in the crack."

Miss Ivy shook her head, wondering if she'd heard right, then changed the subject.

"If you hungry, wash up extra good."

When the men came inside, Calvin running upstairs and Jasper snatching a jelly toast from LeDawn's fingers, Miss Ivy put more bread in the toaster.

She'd known Jasper since he and Calvin were running the streets with a football and long before he met a girl named Queen and brought over a daughter called after the morning sun. Cradling that precious baby, she pictured his other beautiful girls, Nzinga and Shaka, and thought, "A good name helps just so much." Then she touched wood so her words wouldn't be a curse and laid her hands like a blessing on the tiny forehead.

Jasper shook his head at LeDawn shoving toast in her mouth before he could take it.

"Miss Ivy, you know kids eat you out of house and home if you let 'em."

"Then let 'em," she said.

Coming into the kitchen like a cat on soft paws, Calvin slipped Jasper something Miss Ivy wasn't supposed to see. Of course, she saw. She saw everything. This was more serious than a little weed.

"Her mama know what you two up to?"

Calvin wasn't having it. "Not your business, Aunt Itch."

"Why he call her that?" LeDawn asked her daddy, but there was no reply.

No one living knew where the nickname came from, so Miss Ivy let Calvin go on believing what she figured he told Jasper. Poison ivy. The way it was everywhere, like her nose getting in his business. He sniffed the air.

"You a fine one to talk. Pot calling the kettle black." His dark eyes narrowed. "And where you getting it from?"

"Charlie been by," Miss Ivy snapped. "And y'all need to get up out my kitchen." She touched LeDawn's thin shoulder. "Not you."

But they were leaving. Calvin waited for Jasper and the girl to go out before he took a parting shot. "Least you got Charlie, huh? Ain't nobody else can stand you no more."

The next Saturday LeDawn stood on the threshold, hopping from foot to foot, then ran for the toilet. When she came out, Miss Ivy, making up a bed in a corner of the living room, saw her shirt, same one as last week, wrinkled and dirty.

"You hungry?"

"Daddy said I can't eat with you no more."

"He say why?"

She glanced from the TV screen to Miss Ivy. "He say he don't want you thinking he don't feed me and . . . "

"And?"

"And you too mean."

Miss Ivy checked through the curtains. Her nephew and Jasper were huddled beside a car with tinted windows. When she turned with a hmpf, she avoided looking at the ashtray on the coffee table. Her entire body hurt but she didn't dare light up, not in front of the town crier.

"He say anything else?"

"No. But when Daddy told me to hold it, Calvin say for me to come inside."

"That was good of him, baby. You come in this house anytime you need."

LeDawn wiped her nose on her sleeve. "He say Aunt Itch looking real bad and probably won't be around long."

Miss Ivy pinched the remains of yesterday's reefer with a bobby pin and lit up. Then closing her eyes and sinking into the pillows, she held on. When she opened them, exhaling the curse of that terrible nickname, LeDawn was plugging her nose.

"It's okay," the little girl said. "It smell like my house in here. My mommy and her friend be smoking all the time."

Miss Ivy wasn't so low-down she would criticize LeDawn's mama. Especially since Calvin was right about her being a hypocrite. She had smoked on and off her whole life, and lately, because her pain medicine was constipating, had turned to a home remedy. She yawned, deciding she wouldn't mind a nap.

"You go on back to your friend," she told LeDawn, who batted her doe eyes like she didn't understand. Miss Ivy laughed. "You already forgot about your lady in the crack?"

"I ain't forgot, Miss Ivy. She say I can have my own room and all the toys I want but . . . "

"But what?"

"I like it better in here. With you."

Well, didn't that melt Miss Ivy's heart? She'd been a lonely child herself, sometimes with just a Raggedy Sue to talk to.

"If you staying, bring that jar from the shelf so we can have us some candy while we watch cartoons."

When LeDawn paused to stare at a framed photo of an infant, Miss Ivy hurried up and added, "Watch you don't drop it," before she could ask if it was Calvin. For wasn't the girl nosy? A pile of wrappers between them, she kept talking between bites. "Why you got a bed down here?"

"Case I feel like watching TV all night," Miss Ivy replied with a light laugh. She gave LeDawn a poke and made her giggle. "Maybe I'll invite you for a pajama party."

"What about Charlie?" she asked timidly. "Won't Charlie be mad?"

Charlie? "Now why you say that?"

"My mama's boyfriend say he don't like noise."

Miss Ivy sucked hard on a piece of peppermint. "Just us," she said when she trusted herself not to cuss. "Just us girls." As the men came inside, she cracked it between her teeth. They were in high spirits.

"How you doin' Miss Ivy?" Jasper asked while he helped himself to candy. He glanced at the bed. "You doin' okay?"

"We gonna have a pajama party," LeDawn squealed. "Right, Miss Ivy? Just us girls."

She opened her eyes late next morning, embarrassed to see LeDawn's thin face drawn down in worry. The poor thing had circles under her eyes and because she was chewing the right side of her lip, the left drooped like she had Bell's Palsy. Miss Ivy had a vision of how trenches would frame her mouth one day, and worry lines carve themselves permanently in her forehead. "Black don't crack," she thought to herself, "but it can pucker and wrinkle same as this old cotton sheet." She pulled herself up to sit on the side of the bed, patting a spot.

"You riding around with your Daddy on Sundays now?"

"My mama not feeling good," LeDawn said, scooching over until their hips touched. "I hope she not gonna die too."

Miss Ivy drew in a quick breath. "Ain't nobody dying, baby. Not me, not your mama . . . nobody."

"That's not what Calvin say."

"What he say today?"

"He say the doctor give you a few weeks, but you don't believe her."

"He say all that?"

"Yep. He say he don't know where he gonna live when you drop dead."

Miss Ivy's mouth sighed. From the mouth of babes. She had raised Calvin since he was twelve, like he was her own son. She dared a quick glance at the frame. They'd had a few dustups, but now she knew what Calvin really thought of her.

"It late. Why you still in bed, Miss Ivy? Must have been somethin' real good on TV last night."

Miss Ivy couldn't help smiling. She even laughed when LeDawn tried to bounce. The mattress was hard as a rock.

"You hungry?"

By the time Miss Ivy shuffled into the kitchen with a walker, the purse with her pain medicine and checkbook strung over the front, LeDawn was on the footstool, washing at the sink. The basin was covered in little pebbles and when she turned LeDawn's hands over to inspect, she was shocked by the indentations in her palms.

"How you get this dirty?"

"Listening," LeDawn whispered.

"You talking to your friend again?"

LeDawn shrank back, almost like she was scared of being hit, so Miss Ivy let her eat in peace. Without much of an appetite herself, she nibbled dry toast and tried not to be bothered by piggish slurps and swallows. After a second bowl of cereal, the child lifted her eyes like cups of clear water.

"I won't leave you," she said.

"What's that?"

But Jasper and Calvin had come into the house, passing like a couple of thieves up the stairs. She hated to do it, but thought she might ask Calvin to help her to the toilet and back to bed. Only she didn't have a chance to speak to him alone.

"Hurry up and hug Miss Ivy goodbye," Jasper told LeDawn as they headed out again, this time chests high like Wall Street bankers.

Good thing Miss Ivy was sitting. Otherwise she would have been bowled over by that hug. Still holding tight, the girl asked if she might tell a secret, and flashing back to the nasty dancing, Miss Ivy's blood froze. *Please don't let this child tell me somebody abusing her.* She forced herself not to shout.

"Sure you can, honey."

"I got a plan so you ain't gotta die."

Miss Ivy, poorly as she was doing, and feeling ganged up on, didn't mean to, immediately wished she hadn't, but she pushed LeDawn away.

"I already told you, ain't nobody gonna die! Now go on before your daddy get mad."

Later she tried to forget the conversation by telling herself children are forgiving by nature. She knew it was a lie because she never forgave her grandmother for the terrible nickname. In the meantime, the pain behind her temple flared up. It was so bad by Wednesday, Calvin had to drive her to the appointment.

"Ask the doctor for something stronger," he kept saying in the car. "And lots of it."

Miss Ivy, who had been coming up short on her count, was glad he waited in the car. With all the talk on television about people abusing drugs, she felt ashamed, weak—guilty even—when she asked for something to help. She was surprised at how quickly Dr. Patel agreed and didn't get down from the examining table when she had the prescription in her hand.

"What other treatment option I got?"

Dr. Patel opened her mouth, then shut it a few seconds. "Ivy, what I'm trying to say is, we're out of options. It's time to go home. Enjoy the time you have left."

Miss Ivy was floating. It was the most wonderful feeling in the world, until the scritch-scratch started. Now whose hand messing with me under the covers, she thought, and squeezing her thighs together went stiff as a plank.

"Stop that!" she called out when the scratching became a slow crawl up her belly.

"Got your own map of the world," a lodger in her head buzzed back. "With titties high as Kilimanjaro."

Except there were no mountains. "Not anymore," she told the lodger, who was, of course, her grandmother. "I'm flat as old Mulberry Street."

For with her baby's death, the map scratched into flesh during the eighth month of pregnancy was a map to nowhere: its mountains useless and doomed to shrivel and fall long before they were scraped entirely away.

She pushed away an image of her son's eyes, only two days old, and their light disappearing like a stone in the ocean. The place his small face had occupied was instantly filled with waves of shame: Calvin getting her on and off the toilet. Wiping her behind. Propping her up to take a pill.

A few times she tried to tell him not to worry because she was leaving him the house and the little money in the bank, but her tongue was thick and useless.

"You're gonna be alright, Miss Ivy," a different voice whispered.

Unable to speak, she answered in her head. "If you an angel of the Lord, I'm ready for you to take me."

Not having been in church, well or sick, in years, she sounded ridiculous to herself. She had refused visits from her parents' old pastor and offers of food so often that no one offered anymore. The sin of pride. She wondered if the angel knew.

But the cooing voice began to chop up like a bad phone connection and stopped.

"It's me, Miss Ivy."

"That you, LeDawn? You hungry?"

"You ain't have to get out of bed. Daddy say he take me to McDonald's if I be good. Can I tell you something?"

"Yes," Miss Ivy said, for despite what she'd told the angel, she was relieved to be earthbound. The thought of salty french fries straight out of the fryer was stirring an appetite. "Whatever it is, you can tell Miss Ivy."

"The crack in the sidewalk," she whispered. "The lady say, 'Where you at, girl? You need to come on.'"

"Well, that's heaven, I guess." Miss Ivy sighed. "'And a little child shall lead us.'"

"No, no," LeDawn said, screwing up her face. "The woman say *home*. She say, 'You come on home and have a nice supper, with pie.' And I say, 'I love pie, but please-please can I bring my friend Miss Ivy?'"

Miss Ivy laughed. It was a long speech for a little girl with a crooked mouth. "And how I'm supposed to get up from this bed and walk into a crack for a piece of pie?"

"I don't know, Miss Ivy but we figure it out."

Miss Ivy was enjoying herself. "And what she say about me tagging along?"

So serious now. Quiet. All she needed was glasses, Miss Ivy decided, and this child would be a dead ringer for Shirley Chisholm. She nudged her side to make her smile, but it was no use.

"What kind of pie you say it was?"

"I don't know, but I told her we go together—me and you. I said, 'I ain't leave my friend Miss Ivy.'"

"Then come find me tomorrow," Miss Ivy said more gently. "We check that crack together our own selves."

But there was no LeDawn the next day, or the next week, or the next month. Calvin mentioned that Jasper got himself caught by the police and was out of commission for a while. The whole business had to cool down.

"Who's taking care of LeDawn?"

He shrugged. "She got a mama. Queen just mad Jasper can't pay child support."

Miss Ivy started feeling better after Thanksgiving. She felt so good she had Calvin bring the Christmas tree down from the attic and move her back upstairs. She threw a quilt over the bed so it would stop spooking her and went shopping for a brown-skinned baby doll for LeDawn. The kind her grandmother would never buy.

Calvin enjoyed telling her how Queen took the gift without saying thank you or calling LeDawn. He described a house stinking of reefer.

"Worse than up in here," he teased.

He never saw the girl the whole time, although there was a thump-thumping from the second floor. The place was packed.

"Wouldn't be surprised if your Charlie was there."

Miss Ivy ignored the insinuation. "Well, I did my best," she said, and Calvin had the decency to stop grinning and nod his head. For the sake of her own health, she let it go.

De-stressing helped. At an appointment in February, she didn't ask for a new prescription and was annoyed when the doctor wrote it up anyhow.

"I'll be honest with you," Dr. Patel said. "A remission like yours is not uncommon."

Late March, nobody around to laugh, she limped out of the house without her cane. She had lost a lot of weight, so despite a general weakness from sitting on the couch all winter, she was more mobile than she'd been. Just slow, clinging to the railing of the ramp. The sunlight pricked at the headache above her left eye, but busy enjoying the buds on the trees and inspecting the garden bed, she ignored it.

"Crocus!" she called to the purple tongues poking through the matted leaves.

There was a small crack in the sidewalk where LeDawn had danced months before. An ordinary old crack like a thousand others across Mulberry Street. *Ha! How anyone supposed to walk through a crack too narrow for an ant?* Miss Ivy would have given the world to crouch down and put her ear to it. She tapped her foot on the spot.

"Girl!" a voice shouted, making her almost fall over. "Where you at, girl?"

Miss Ivy looked around. There was nobody close by.

"Girl! Girl!" The voice was rubber, bouncing from one back yard to another, and it gave her the sweats because if that was LeDawn's lady with pie, there was likely a licking on top instead of vanilla ice cream. It reminded her of her grandmother's, a voice cloaked in sugar and spice. But there was more often pain than treat, for Grandma was a trickster and quick with slipper, swatter, and magazine.

"Itchy fingers," she shouted between strikes. "See if I can't beat the thief out of you!"

Miss Ivy climbed the ramp with a worse headache for her troubles, each step a struggle with the rubber tongue of a busted sole. When she stopped to gather strength for the last few feet, the past caught up with her.

"Itch!"

Whenever the old woman misplaced something or something went missing, usually food, a frequent occurrence in a house full of Grands dropped off in waves thick as locust, she shouted the cruel nickname. Itch, short for itchy fingers. Picked up by the cousins, a foil to their own larceny, it followed little Ivy like dog shit on the bottom of her shoes. Sent to the corner, forgotten while the others fed, she became expert as a mouse at finding the leavings, the pinches, the crumbs, and the coatings. It didn't matter that she was the skinniest because that only made Grandma angrier. She forced turpentine down Ivy's throat and woke her for a humiliating inspection by flashlight. Unfazed by the absence of any "thieving tapeworms" in Ivy's drawers, Grandma laid a curse: "Once a thief, always a thief."

Jasper got out of jail the Monday after Palm Sunday. The following Saturday he came by the house with a bouquet of flowers for Miss Ivy. He looked in far better shape. Pimples cleared up. Thick muscles under his short sleeves.

"You look good," she said. Calvin was a shrimp beside him.

"That's what four months of cafeteria food will do," he said with a boyish grin. "And basketball. You look good too, Miss Ivy."

She felt her cheeks flush. "How's my little friend?" she said quickly. "Why you didn't bring her?"

"Me and her mama ain't talkin no more. She got a new *friend*."

"Try to bring her tomorrow," Miss Ivy said. "I want to give her an Easter basket."

By the time Calvin came down to breakfast, a ham was in the oven, greens were simmering, and Miss Ivy was humming over the potato salad while the coconut cake cooled. The pastor had called with an eleventh-hour offer to have her picked up for service and she had almost said yes. Almost. But she didn't want to rush getting dressed and fixing one of her wigs. Didn't want to miss the look on LeDawn's face at what was waiting in the living room.

Then Calvin showed his true colors and spoiled the good feeling. She turned off the greens and put the oven down and went upstairs to bed.

"Where she at?" she heard Jasper shouting. "I smell ham but where Miss Ivy."

"Jasper here," Calvin said a few moments later through her closed door.

"Tell him I'm doing poorly."

"He got LeDawn. They got her dressed up for Easter."

Words didn't come easy. She forced herself to tell Jasper he looked good in his pressed shirt, then pretended LeDawn was in her Sunday best instead of a dress two sizes too small and hair half done like her mama ran out of grease and energy. Miss Ivy's nose pricked at the smell of fried food and weed, and when she got a close look at those ashy knees, she couldn't stay quiet.

"If those were chicken legs, we'd need a pan of gravy."

LeDawn's eyes flickered at the mention of chicken and gravy and again when Miss Ivy led her into the living room for the store-bought basket with a yellow ribbon on top. Through the cellophane you could see a coloring book and crayons, a stuffed rabbit, and whole lot of candy, but LeDawn shrugged and left it on the coffee table beside the ashtray. Another letdown in a day Miss Ivy had wanted to be perfect.

She glared at the Rose Bowl Parade five minutes before she sent Le-Dawn to the bathroom for hair grease, a comb, and Vaseline, and with the child on the floor between her knees, fixed two pretty braids tied together with the yellow ribbon. After she finished the edges, proud of the neat little head in front of her, she celebrated with a couple tokes, glad LeDawn stayed glued to Mickey Mouse.

"How your mama?"

"She alright."

"I been out to see your crack."

"Huh?"

"The crack in the sidewalk you told me about." She turned down the volume. "I may have heard your friend."

LeDawn shrugged, eyes glued to the screen. "I don't like her no more."

"You still doing your little dance?"

"Mama's friend say it make his head hurt."

Miss Ivy rubbed the side of her own head and recalled how the argument with Calvin started. She had her back to him, arranging eggs on the salad. She must have paused to massage her temple because he told her to call the doctor.

"I'm done with doctors," she said.

When she turned around, wondering at his silence, there was a baggie of reefer in front of him on the table. She watched him fluff the bag like a pillow, then taking a pinch, roll a skinny joint.

With a catch in her throat, she told him, "Probably just a spring cold."

"Get stronger painkillers," he said, rolling another. "Something for the headache."

"Maybe you what giving me a headache," she snapped, trying not to cry. "Disrespecting my house."

He used the joint to point to her purse on the walker. "Disrespect, huh? I give you two of these for one. Unless your *Charlie* comin by."

"He probably will," she said turning back to the unfinished salad. "Probably stopping by for some of this ham."

"When he do, tell him I put a lock on my door because somebody got itchy fingers."

She'd given in to Calvin. Had had no choice. But now, despite his victory, he looked irritated when she shuffled out of the house, holding the railing with one hand, LeDawn with the other, not trusting her own feet. Miss Ivy knew exactly how she looked with a housedress falling like a circus tent and the face of a hundred-year-old granny instead of forty-nine. She hoped she didn't look high because it felt like there was something extra in his weed. Something taking her out of her body and into the air. She was hungry all of a sudden too, and thought of the ham in the oven that needed turning up and the greens still tough on top of the stove. She didn't have time to be out here with LeDawn and that silly crack but things were in motion she couldn't stop. Not even to be bothered by the men's banter.

"Damn it, man," Calvin was saying. "You need to start feeding that girl."

"That's on her mama," Jasper grumbled, avoiding Miss Ivy's face as she passed, pulling the child to the spot she remembered seeing the crack.

"I'm sure it was here," she said. "You remember where it was, Le-Dawn? Why you don't try that little dance of yours."

But LeDawn only shook her head, and when her daddy said let's go, climbed into the back seat without a goodbye. "Just like your mama," Miss Ivy thought bitterly, her head pounding. "Ain't got manners to first."

She needed Calvin's help back inside, but he was striding in the opposite direction. More afraid of being seen than wanting help, she gripped her own self around the waist and willed the earth to open and swallow her whole.

"Miss Ivy, Miss Ivy!" It was Jasper.

LeDawn climbed out of the car and looked both ways before crossing.

"Forgot the Easter Basket," Jasper hollered, the car already rolling away. "Imma swing around the block a few minutes and be back. When that ham supposed to be ready?"

Miss Ivy clung to the hand extended to take her inside, but LeDawn froze, staring bug-eyed at the sidewalk, and shook her arm. The little crack had parted like lips.

"Wait here, Miss Ivy," she said excitedly. "I'll get the candy and we go together."

But in those few moments, as LeDawn tore into the house, a lady's voice lifted from the crack.

"Come on, Child. Time to come home."

"I'm waiting on my friend," Miss Ivy pleaded , disguising her voice to be high and squeaky like LeDawn's. "I'm waiting for Miss Ivy."

"Last chance," the lady sang. "Only enough sugar and spice for one."

It might be trickery, or it might not, but the air was pie.

"Don't try me, Girl."

"But Miss I—"

"I ain't gonna ask but one last time."

"Please!"

"What I say?"

"Yes, ma'am!" she chirped—and turning from LeDawn, who was running towards her full tilt, the basket so big it nearly covered the disappointment in her face, Miss Ivy stepped into the crack.

KEEPING UP

Jackie couldn't hardly keep up with his big sister's pace along the narrow footpath crisscrossed by tree roots quick to trip him and low hanging branches sharp as nails across his cheeks. He knew about Hansel and Gretel and didn't doubt that she, who had picked and poked at him as long as he'd been breathing, wouldn't hesitate to leave him behind in the deepest, darkest part of the forest. Harboring snakes big around as a man's arm, it was a place where even Grandpa, who hunted these woods, couldn't find him. Luckily, Buss Ward ran along, darting off the path to chase a chipmunk but never failing to rush back from somewhere ahead, tripping up Jackie's feet in his excitement.

One while though, Jackie called and called but Buss Ward didn't come. Thinking he was lost but good, he stumbled like a drunkard, huffing and puffing until he found Nell by the side of the path, trapping his dog in her arms. He plopped down out of range, hiding his tear-stained face in his elbow.

"You bes' keep up."

He knew to keep quiet. Not to say anything irritating in the heat because she was a bull when her musk rose. Buss Ward knew it too and, wiggling free, went to lie on the cool grass.

"Somethin' chasing you, l'il brother," Nell said plainly. "And it mean to kill you."

He studied her face. She looked like Mama did when he had a bellyache. Genuinely sorry. But Nell could be one of those Hollywood actresses, everybody said, so he stayed mum.

"I make up lot of stories, right?"

He nodded.

"This ain't one of those." She opened her arms, offering him the spot Buss Ward had vacated. "Move closer, so you don't get snatched before I finish."

He bolted into what he hoped wasn't a trap. Risked his life, because Nell, bony where Mama was soft, was capable of murder. He pretended not to sniff for the soap smell under her sticky skin.

"What this somethin' want with me?"

"Nothing in particular," she said very knowledgably. "Maybe it just enjoy a good meal of a scaredy cat now and then."

He tried to pull away, but she had him tight. "I ain't a scaredy cat."

"I ain't said you were. But you know how I be listening to Daddy and them?"

"Uhu."

"Well, Daddy say this somethin' so bad, so downright dirty, it make a grown man pee his pants and cry for his mama."

"I ain't gonna cry. I ain't gonna pee my pants." His boast sounded hollow out here in the woods, and he was suddenly alert, like Buss Ward late at night, his nose in the air and tail stuck straight out as they heard the scrape of Daddy easing the rifle out from under the bed. This serious Nell, this Nell who held him, was like the rifle in Daddy's hands. Dangerous. Any minute she could paralyze him in a half nelson, then twist her fist into his armpit, pulsing pain through his helpless body like electricity.

"Ain't no such thing," he protested softly.

"Poor Jackie."

"I ain't gonna cry! I ain't gonna pee!"

This time the words flew out fully throated, flushed like a pheasant trying to escape death as it flew straight towards it. Jackie fought Nell's grip. He kicked his heels into the ground, sputtering and stuttering that she was k-k-killing him, and when no amount of pleading helped, he went limp.

She shook him like she used to do her Raggedy Sue, then almost seemed to cradle him. Her voice was softer. "Listen, Jackie. I can't protect you if you can't keep up."

"Why it want me?" he whimpered.

There was a clipping tacked to Grandpa's wall about a girl hit by a thunderbolt out of the clear sky. Why it chose her long plaits bound with white ribbons? Her Sunday smile? No one had an answer, but he kept asking, like he did now.

"What I do?"

It happened fast. He worked to keep the pain out of his face until Nell, looking pleased that he didn't cry, stopped pinching a chunk of his bare leg.

"Not cause you ugly," she said. She bit her lip. "And not cause you a scaredy cat."

"So, what is it?"

"It's like this, Jackie. You gonna be a big man . . . like Daddy and them all. And you Black."

"Black?" The word came out like a squeak.

"That's all it is. And no way around it."

She jumped to her feet and was off. She may have slowed a bit. Jackie was keeping up.

ASHE

At sixty-five Pat still thinks about Mama and Daddy every day. They were killed decades before The Fire, but her memories of the two events are scrambled.

As she scoots along the bench after Iris, her cousin Cap and his son Gary position themselves in the row behind. She avoids eye contact with the crowd filling the gallery, many of them former neighbors. Whenever *The Lost Tribe* comes together, a blaze rekindles in their eyes. Born of rage and confusion, it's a fever that doesn't break. But then there's that young woman, Altaira, who always sits in the middle of the gallery. When they passed in the lobby, Pat saw blue extensions braided into her hair like a feathered headdress. The week before it was a fresh tattoo, the area around her shoulder raised and angry. Pat thought it was another bleeding heart, but Cap said it was a bat.

"Why would someone with pretty skin spoil it like that?" He was upset, so she told him it was probably a way around the ban on "provocative messaging" on T-shirts and hoodies.

Pat waves up to the gallery, and Altaira flashes back a rare smile. It must be for Iris's sake. Her husband, the "Felix" bannered below her collarbones, hasn't been seen since the night of The Fire.

A guilty verdict has already been reached. Today, after a nearly four-week trial and almost two years to the day after Mulberry Street was burned to the ground, John Bullock, Iris's grandson who calls her Mama, is going

78

to be sentenced for vehicular manslaughter, stemming from road rage, and inciting a riot.

Iris has gotten smaller over the course of the trial. She'd disappear into the wooden bench if Pat didn't sit up straight and hold her hand. But to do that, to be a rock for her friend, Pat has to ignore the belly pain she's lived with her whole life. Her mother used to call it belly talk, a source of African wisdom she ought to listen to. But Daddy said belly talk wasn't magical, and even though she was little when he explained why, she hasn't forgotten.

When the lawyer met them outside this morning, he assured Iris there was still hope the judge would show compassion.

"Justice is blind, Mrs. Bullock. You have to keep believing that."

Iris managed to smile at his kind words, but Pat felt pain shoot up from her navel. Her father was right. Proximity to white people could be ulcer-producing.

She saw his point clear enough yesterday. As the prosecutor's final statement railed on and on, she watched the lawyer. Was he checking his watch because he had somewhere else to be? Somewhere more important than helping John and Iris? Surely he could read the judge's round red face without the commentary of Pat's belly. He should have been straight with Iris and told her the judge was going to throw the book at her sun and moon. And then, if he really believed in justice, he should have said he was going to fight and keep fighting. That he had an appeal already planned out.

White people. The police who killed her parents, the legal system that saw Black people as guilty until proven innocent, the lawyers that cashed the check, and the newspaper owners who buried the story on the obituary page while Family Services took their sweet time placing her with Aunt Sue to be adopted.

Aunt Sue kept a scrapbook, so she has the sketchy details at her fingertips and knows there's a sad irony to the public failing to do something. In the years since, their deaths have repeated so many times that these details—their names and ages, for instance, the age and gender of their surviving child, their place of residence (the old house three blocks up from Mulberry)—don't make them special.

Jolted back to the courtroom by the judge's gavel, she leans into Gary's hands on her shoulder and breathes. Who wouldn't mind a belly with a little superhero inside telling you not to go out for Skittles, not to play in the park, not to tell the white officer you have a legal permit for the gun in your glove compartment? Not to go to work and school, not to doze on the couch in case a racist plans to burn your house down and blame your neighbor. Not to act like you got some rights. She takes an antacid from her purse and offers one to Iris, along with a fresh tissue.

"Don't fuss over me, Pat. We just got to keep the faith."

Pat doesn't need a hurting stomach to tell her what she sees coming a mile away. She saw it when the lawyer let her testimony to John's character be mocked by the prosecutor. She saw it in the gnarled fingers of poor old Mavis Jenkins, speaking in the ancient language of Mulberry Street, what Aunt Sue called flat. If anyone had genuine visions, it was the eighty-pound woman speaking through loose dentures. Cross-examined by the prosecution, her wise counsel, like an ancient scroll exposed to light, was turned to dust.

"Tell us what you saw, Miss Jenkins. In the days leading up to the fire, describe for the jury what you saw in the area of your home."

"I seen little silver UFOs buzzing around my flowers."

["Order!"]

"And what did you do when you saw those flying objects?"

"I says, 'Lawd Jesus! You gots to do *sumpin* up around here.'"

["Order!"]

The prosecutor made a little pivot toward the jury, making sure they were in on the joke. "And why do you think UFOs came to your yard, specifically, Miss Jenkins? Did they offer you a message?"

["Order!"]

Could her eyes get any bigger? "Of course, they did."

["Order!"]

"And what is that message?"

"Judgement Day."

"And what does Judgement Day mean, precisely?"

"The End Time, naturally."

Instead of immediately hammering for order, the judge cupped his mouth to hide a smile, and most of the jury and lawyers tried not to chuckle, while neighbors who had known her gentle ministering of roses sniffled, and those who had heard her sing a loved one home to *His Eye Is On The Sparrow* were devastated. The next-oldest of the old were powerless to protect their mad historian and social commentator, their songbird, their prophet, their last link to a mama and papa who'd raised them up talking exactly like her.

The worst came next. Her testimony, though ridiculed, was used to corroborate the charge that from inside jail John Bullock had incited Black men to burn down the neighborhood, then blamed white people in order to start a race war.

"Ma'am, on the afternoon of the fire, did you see people in your yard?"

"I surely did."

"And to your recollection, were these men white?"

"No sir, they were not. Them devils was black with noses stuck out like pigs."

Pat watched the whole trial like theater and knows there was nothing she could have said to change the outcome: when they give John the maximum, good, dear Iris is going to fall out.

Aunt Sue had a solid insurance policy. After she died, Cap and them joined her in the house on Mulberry Street, while Willie and his wife got a place a few blocks down. Aunt Sue wasn't a nice person, and London, Willie's boy, resembles her in the worst way: a bully and stingy to boot. "Don't make me ask twice," she catches him telling the other kids. For toys, for money. Even as a baby he could smell a penny in the corner of your pocket. She tried to talk sense into his head, and he listened to Gary some, but Cap was Cap, quick to slip a sulking child a dollar bill in place of a stern word.

"Man needs more than jingling change in his pocket."

Even as a child, Gary understood how to save, but over and over London smashed piggy banks and showed his long face to Cap for a reward.

A day before the road rage incident, she was frying fish when the boy came to the back door huffing and puffing. With Gary in college, she was trying to discover London's redeeming qualities, but in that moment couldn't list one. The food she would gladly make for her favorite went down this one's gullet like fattening a duck. And worse, she always has to pry a thank you out of him when even his tight-lipped mama can manage a grudging compliment, "He won't eat nobody's cooking but Aunt Pat's." She was tempted to hide the whiting in the oven to teach him a lesson, but it wasn't in her nature. Nor was whipping a child, although she wasn't above a threat.

"I will fuck him up!" London said, pumping his fists in the air. A sickening duplicate of his daddy, only with this one she has the upper hand.

"Stop talking like that before I get my belt. And tell me what you did now."

"What I did? Old white man, Aunt Pat. Called me a nigger."

For the first time, she saw tears coming from this hardheaded child as he became more and more incoherent. It took ten minutes to untangle the story from his broken mouth. How he'd been *innocently* taking a shortcut through the yards between Mulberry Street and Cypress. How he'd barely stepped on the white man's yard when the man called him *a nigger*.

"Ain't nobody ever called me that, Aunt Pat. Ever."

Pat's heart was racing. "Slow down, London. Take another breath." With London, there is always more to the story than what you hear. Sometimes it's an out-and-out lie. "What you do to the man?"

"What *I* do, Aunt Pat?" He gave her the side-eye. "I swear to God, Aunt Pat. I was doing nothing."

She should have told his parents, but she doesn't talk to either of them. She and Willie got a six-foot rule and Miss Thing makes no secret she thinks Cap and them got more money from Aunt Sue's policy. Talking to total strangers was easier, even white ones. So, after she drove London home, she stopped by the dilapidated red house he pointed out. One of those zombie properties landlords snatch up for a few bucks. When no one answered the bell, she followed the sound of an electric saw around back, squeezing her belly between a hedge and an extra wide pickup.

Two white men her age were watching a younger man in a wife beater cut up a tree. She was just lifting her hand for attention when a dog charged and about gave her a heart attack. It couldn't reach her because of the chain around its neck, but her knees buckled, and smelling fear, the dog tore up the dirt like it wanted to eat her alive. The man turned off his saw.

"What's up?"

On top of containing a war between fight and flight, her stomach, digesting hot sauce and whiting, was knotted with anger and worry. But Pat stood her ground, determined to get to the bottom of things. Because of London's history of lying, she was very careful.

"My nephew says you two had words this morning."

"Nephew, huh?" The man sat the saw on a stump. She could see the bits of wood chewed in the blade and rolled back on the balls of her feet. "You mean that brat stealing my lunch, right out my truck?"

Now why would London do a thing like that? A boy who only eats in Aunt Pat's kitchen. It had to be a lie. She straightened her shoulders and squared her feet, pretending she didn't hear the dog growl a warning.

"That's not what he says. Says you called him out his name."

The man scratched the back of his head and turned to the men, kee-keeing into their fists. "Sorry ma'am, but your kid's lying. I told him to stay off my property before I call the cops. That was the end of it."

Cops? Pat felt her sugar drop. "Kids been cutting through these yards for years."

The man mopped his face with the bottom of his shirt and came closer. Keeping the dog in the corner of her eye, she could see the yellow under his armpits, smell his funk.

"Well, you see," he said. "This is my yard and anybody think about taking a shortcut, needs to think twice."

"He's in third grade."

"Yeah? I coulda called the cops. Still might."

She was lightheaded. Something of sulfur and stone twisting in her belly. The man returned to the saw and revved it back to life, and the dog, sensing he wanted her gone, began barking and pulling, unconcerned with the chain digging into its thick neck. It was as she was turning to leave that she saw the white swastika spray-painted on the back of the house. It had to be twice her five feet and wider than arms' length.

"Tell him to stay the fuck off my property," the man shouted as she hurried around the truck. She had her keys out and wished she had the nerve to dig them into the paint. Did she have the nerve?

By the time she got to her car, she was doubled over with pain and remorse. She didn't have the nerve.

Early next morning, she was on the porch in her house slippers and scarf. Her belly, still five years old in a middle-aged body, whined and stomped in a fit that coffee was making worse. She tossed nearly a full cup into the yard and decided to talk to Cap as soon as he woke up. He knew people in the mayor's office. Someone would know what to do about a swastika showing up in the neighborhood and a racist threatening to call the police on London.

"Morning!" It was John, across the street, having a cigarette before work. He smiled. "That house number of yours came out again."

"That's good, that's good, John."

He *was* a good man and like a son to Cap long before he and Gary dominated high school sports. London, whose heroes mostly came flying out of comic books, idolized him because as gentle as John was, all 6'3", he had once been a warrior in the defender spot.

They were interrupted by a truck racing up the block, a Confederate flag waving from the bed as it passed. "What the fuck!" John hollered. He stepped into the street, staring into the empty space where the truck disappeared. She came down her steps, telling him about the driver, the swastika on the side of his house, and about London, when they heard it coming around again, John in direct line of being run over before she screamed. Had he already intended to take chase? Had good, calm John, reached his breaking point?

Witnessing from the porch and paralyzed with fear, Pat was tongue-tied but not her belly. Naw. It didn't moan and groan and cramp up inside. Not this time. Didn't double her over. Didn't lose its nerve. For once and always it spoke clear as day, and damn if it didn't cry out to John like a little girl, "Make him stop!"

John stands for the sentencing. At no point during the trial did he mention being with her on the street that morning. Never pointed to her and said, "She told me to do it." And when called to testify, Pat neglected to mention the outburst from her belly. Like anyone would have believed her. They hadn't believed in the swastika. Or the threats against London. The prosecutor told the jury that Pat's history with the police had radicalized her.

"Transformed by an accident sixty years ago, she has harbored a grudge against white people ever since."

She is John's unofficial godmother.

"A teacher and role model for his radical beliefs."

She holds Iris's scarred hand, the brown peeled away to a permanent white streaked with pink, and recalls two angels, their Afros gleaming, taking her by the hand from the couch to the front door and into the street. She's one of the few survivors without a scar.

Except for London, angry that children aren't allowed, and Cap's wife Fredonia who says her heart can't relive that night, her family has come together. Willie, his eyes shifting with the rage and shame he will always carry, avoids her, but listens alongside his wife from their seats by the exit, while Gary's hands stay firmly on her shoulders. Cap stays close to Iris.

Twenty years for vehicular manslaughter to be served consecutively with ten years for inciting a riot. It sounds like the roof of the courtroom is on fire. There's a wail from the gallery and Pat, struggling to hold Iris, knows, without looking, that it's Altaira. Cap wedges his hands under Iris's arms as her head flops forward. She will have to be carried out.

The judge threatens to have people arrested if they don't quit hollering. "Do you have any last statements?" he asks John in the sudden quiet.

Pat hates him. The way he probably thinks they're quiet because of his gavel and his robe. He doesn't know Mulberry Street people. They've seen enough of police and jail for a lifetime. And one more thing. They want to hear John speak.

"I take full responsibility," he says. Same soft-spoken John. Nothing else.

With John's words, the last embers seem to go out. Ash, Pat thinks to herself, remembering the way it sticks to your skin forever. But from deep inside, her belly replies, "Ashe," and the courtroom erupts again.

THE MAGICAL NEGRO

Altaira!

Someone tackled me from behind. Rolled me until the flames went out, then stood me rudely on my feet. I was in too much shock to cry out or resist, and in the next moment, my arms were wrenched behind me and my wrists clasped in iron. *The police!* My eyesight is usually keen but the swiftness of this second assault, compounded by raging fire and smoke in every direction, made seeing faces and badges impossible. One shoved me toward the flashing lights of a cruiser where another waited to corral me into the back seat. "What's the charge?" I said through my burned lips and throat, but there was no reply as the officer sped through the streets.

My house was burning, so why was I being blamed? Why arrested rather than offered medical treatment? The crude methods of care would have been worthless anyhow, but it rankled me that a hurt dog could expect better care. I was angry when I should have been focused on getting my strength back. To heal and find Altaira. She was going to return from class with a pizza for movie night, and finding the house destroyed, assume the worst.

At the public safety building, I was powerless against a body search and a flash that felt like I imagine a blast of radiation would feel. The police replaced my ruined clothes, but the rough fabric was sandpaper against my burns. Because discomfort appeared to give them pleasure, I masked it with a swagger as they herded a group of us into a cell with equally confused and injured men. I recognized a few neighbors with various degrees of burns and battering, many middle-aged and older.

"He look like he supposed to be dead," one of them whispered in my direction. I ignored the comment and turned to a younger man among them.

"What you doing here? What happened?"

I knew Tavarious from the corner. Nice looking with a ready smile. I wasn't a customer, normally, but sometimes Altaira needed something. Now his features rippled with grief and anger.

"Where you been, Negro? They burned the whole goddamn block!" His shouts were answered with curses and moans from the others.

"Who?"

He sucked the back of his teeth like I was the dumbest person he'd ever met. "Them white motherfuckers, man! Mad about they boy dying in the crash."

Altaira had told me about the arrest of our neighbor John Bullock in a road rage incident. Neither of us felt sympathy for the dead truck driver. She'd been right to worry about the consequences.

"Damn cowards," an old man spat out. "I seen them in camouflage out the window and by the time I got 911 on the phone, my roof was burning. When the police finally come through, they snatched *my* black ass."

"I been good my whole life," another senior moaned. "Never thought I'd get my likeness took like some drug-dealing gang banger."

Tavarious laughed like he didn't take the implied insult personally.

"My Mama didn't make it," a boy cried out. He was maybe thirteen but must have been sixteen to be in lockup. Small for his age. He smelled like ivory soap and Vicks VapoRub. A man pulled him close like a child, tucking the boy's head against his heart.

"You don't know for sure, Malcom."

"Naw, I do," Malcolm sniffled. "I was in bed sick when the front of the house blew up. Right at the time my grandmama like to watch her stories."

"Can we pray?" someone called from an adjoining cell, immediately answered with "Shut the fuck up" from a big man in a corner who told him where to stick it.

"Your white Jesus don't give a shit about us."

Him I knew from my late-night habit of smoking on the front stoop. Occasionally we'd light up together and talk about nothing. He'd tell a funny story about driving a city bus, then poke around to find out where I was working. "Between jobs," I'd say. Or "Got a lead on something tomorrow." Never the truth. That I slept all day while Altaira worked, then, after she fell asleep, hit the casino or hustled downtown. He never seemed to judge except the one time he told me I had the prettiest woman on the street and I'd better be prepared for a fight if I fucked things up.

I agreed with him on principle about God, but like the cowed men around me I stared at my blistering hands and arms, afraid to touch my own face, and would have welcomed a savior.

Malcolm's eyes got round and scared. "Anybody see if that lady with the day care make it out with them kids? She my grandmama's best friend."

It got real quiet as we imagined a woman trying to escape the flames and smoke with babies and toddlers. The shock was wearing off. People, lots of people, could be dead.

"Why we in here?" Tavarious screamed through the bars. "Why the fuck we in here and not them motherfuckers who burned us out?"

I left before sunup. The men would wake up with no memory of me or our conversation, but I felt bad leaving them behind.

I holed up in St. Mary's cemetery, not optimal but there were plenty of deer to keep me fed. When I was strong enough, I hunted for bigger prey, the police chief who ordered the arrest of every Black man in a half-mile radius and enough of the arresting officers to make the living feel cursed. Couldn't kill them in one swoop without more reprisals, so I stretched the killing over months. Accidents happened. No witnesses on lone stretches of highway or water. A few lived long enough to die incoherent in hospital.

I lived many lifetimes before The Fire. Afterwards, I became something

I had never been. A stranger to myself, for where my scorched skin blistered and peeled, there was whiteness underneath. Because of the trauma of the metal cuffs, I may never fully heal to the fearsome black creature I once was.

I visited Altaira at the shelter until she moved into an apartment. I would hide in the shadows, listening to her weep, relieved she was alone and despising my selfishness for being relieved. Seeing her face cratered with grief, even in dreams, I wanted to tell her I was still of this world, but that would have been a lie. At the end of my nightly vigil, I returned to the mausoleum, vowing to myself that the visits would end. For both our sakes.

The night I chose to be our last, I marveled at her braids rippling across the pillowcase, envying the woman who had painstakingly plaited as they talked and laughed for hours and hours. She slept deeply, an eye mask shutting out the streetlights, but from time to time, she gasped for air, the result of a frightening habit of holding her breath. My sweet fish out of water.

Lying on her back, her hands clasped over her chest and the sheet fanned out along her spread legs—she always reminded me of a mermaid. Like the one in the fairy tale, she'd sacrificed her true nature to be in my world, with me, and it was time to let her go. Perhaps to my rival on Mulberry Street.

The TV was on. She denied it in the past, but I knew she worried about me out on the streets and used the TV as company. There was a black-and-white movie playing. One I'd never seen. No wonder. Nuns. Then a man appeared on the screen. A Black man, the color of ash among white faces, with flashes of silver across his forehead and cheeks. I caught the gist of the story. He was looking for work. The Mother Superior wanted him to build a chapel, but she couldn't pay him.

I stretched my hand into the light cast by the screen and saw that it and the handsome man were the same color. Perhaps that's why I became caught up in the ridiculous story and watched him bend to the nun's

will. The Fire had filled me with vengeance, made me skeptical of goodness, and yet I was curious about his motivation to work with no recompense. When he slipped away at the end, a decision not unlike my own
planned departure from Altaira, I surprised myself by bursting into sobs.

"Felix? Is that you?"

She was sitting on the side of the bed, her back stooped, her eyes still
covered. I retreated into the shadows to let her think she was still dreaming. Except the movie had left me in a tangle of emotions.

"What happened?" I whispered. "Why did he do it?"

"He didn't. They made him their magical Negro." She smiled, probably remembering I'm averse to magic as much as religion. Smiled like it
was movie night at home on Mulberry Street, having to explain the plots
and characters I frequently misread. A smile instead of surprise or anger
at my reappearance. How many times had she had this dream?

"And what, dear Altaira, is a magical Negro?"

"You, Felix. Here . . . now."

With those words she flew as swiftly as Bela Lugosi across the room,
throwing her weight to knock me off balance, bringing us both down
and pinning me to the floor. No hope for escape because I was under a
spell. The ocean of her braids, a swarm of sea creatures flashing among
them, and the screech as she sank bared teeth into my throat. Something
I would never, had never . . . this was no dream. It was I the quivering
maiden and she, unmasked, the devouring beast.

JENNY

A woman pushed a rattling cart of cans and bottles up the hill. Whenever she listed too far to the right and hit the curb, a runt of a man yelled from twenty yards behind. Then reversing direction and putting her back into the task, she would begin again. Their relationship was complex.

When she'd woken up, some time ago, half drowned, Bud slapped the muck out of her lungs and strapped a makeshift splint to her leg. She couldn't remember her name, so he called her Jenny Gimpy. Love was never mentioned, but wherever she wandered, lost in a fugue, he found her. He showed her how to panhandle. How to fight off competition when he wasn't around. How to stay hydrated in summer and warm in winter. With the acquisition of the shopping cart, their fortunes brightened.

It was around midnight. There had been a Monday holiday. Because trash pickup was a day late, he expanded their territory to hit the early birds. "Hold up!" he hollered, and she stopped between the upper and lower blocks of a cross street, midway along the ascent. She wasn't in the habit of reading street names but "Mulberry" caught her fancy and she began humming. "Do you know the song?" she asked, but huffing and puffing, he ignored her. There were trash cans overflowing with the remnants of celebration. He sent her into the upper block, while he had a smoke.

It's strange how odors on a sweltering night return us to a moment. Rancid milk and chicken guts. The sour bottom of beer cans. The lingering sulfur of fireworks. She stopped humming and sniffed flowers along the front of a blue house, their sweetness pulling her into the yard as careless as a bee. Without thinking, she continued up the side steps and through a screen door to the porch. There was enough light from the street to see a utility box. Dragging it over, she climbed up and ran her hand along the lintel above the house door.

"What the fuck you doing?" It was Bud.

"There's supposed to be a key."

He opened the screen. "You gonna get us shot, fat ass. This ain't your house."

"How you know?"

He pulled her down. "I know because we gotta get the fuck outta here."

She shook him off but followed orders. Hobbled back to the cart, finished the circuit, and rattled and clattered into the lower block.

They never returned to Mulberry Street together. There was just the one time he woke up feverish, humming the tune she'd passed to him like a virus. *Round and Round.* He returned to that house, found the dusty key. Threw it down a drain.

THE CROSSROADS

Mrs. Washington nodded over a bowl of peanuts, dreaming how fine it would be to have a child to keep in her pocket, and when she woke up, there were two, emptying the cupboards and rattling the pots. Not pocket-sized, but small enough to hold together in the crook of one arm, the other arm locked across like the bar of a roller coaster seat, and not worry about them tumbling out of bed. But first she had to catch them.

Summer and Winter were born addicted, so it took a lot of work before they came into themselves. Mrs. Washington pushed a carriage up and down the street all hours of night and day. It rarely stopped the shrieking, but she felt less of a danger out in public. If she snapped, there was a chance someone would hear and stop her in time from choking them.

She was only forty and her hair started to fall out. Then it turned gray. Things only settled after the girls repeated second grade. Mrs. Washington had permanent bald spots by then, but by third grade, they were bringing home certificates galore from MLK Elementary. There was barely space on the refrigerator when they reached fourth grade and got themselves into the gifted program. She bought herself a curly wig for the ceremony. They were the only Black kids on stage.

One afternoon in fifth grade, the fall she was on disability again for her back, they came running home breathless and sweaty. Awakened from a deep nap in front of the TV, Mrs. Washington fussed because doing two of everything included laying two stubborn edges. Also, she

94

hated when they talked loud and fast, one picking up where the other left off. It reminded her how Irene used to get. Stirred up.

"We saw slaves!" Winter was shouting.

"Slow down," Mrs. Washington said, muting the volume. "You saw what?"

Summer took over. "Slaves, Mama! In front of the drugstore."

"Oh, darling. You seen homeless people."

Winter started to put her hands on her hips then thought better of it. "We saw *Roots*, Mama. These were slaves, just like them."

"Runaways," Summer whispered.

Mrs. Washington put her hand to the lever of the recliner and rose up straight. The better to look them in the eye.

"Okay. Imma test you. Did they look hungry?"

"Yep."

"And raggedy?"

"Uhu."

"Ask for money?"

"How you know, Mama?"

She motioned them closer. "How many you see?"

"Three," Winter said. "A mama, daddy, and a little boy."

Summer shook her head. "You didn't see the blanket? The woman had a baby."

Mrs. Washington hushed the argument Summer triggered. "From what you say, you seen a family of homeless folks."

Winter pulled away. "What's the difference, Mama? Don't you gotta help them, like you do that old man?"

"I don't gotta do nothing, but y'all need to get me a glass of water and get out of those school clothes. Now!"

She took a bottle from her robe pocket and broke a tablet in half, keeping it out of sight until the girls were in their room. They left piles of library books on the coffee table, so she knew they'd be back.

The old man. She shivered. Both of them were softhearted, but it was just like Winter to remember something happening way back in July. Something she'd been trying to forget. It started with those soft hearts. Shaming her to do what she normally wouldn't.

"He look sick . . . and hungry."

"Why don't nobody help?"

She was going to ignore the girls and beat the light, but she spotted a cruiser over at McDonald's and hit the brake, stopping at the tip of the island used for turning left across the boulevard's westerly moving lanes. The soul resident of the island, a gray-haired man waving a piece of cardboard with the word *help*, came up to the same height as Mrs. Washington at the wheel. The slightest movement of her neck caused pain in her lower back, but she managed a glimpse of his tattered evening jacket and crushed derby. The round-handled cane in his opposite hand could have been plucked from her grandfather's coat rack.

"Please, Mama. Please!"

The old man craned his neck to see into the back seat, where the girls were pressed to the glass. He gave such a big, toothy smile she was shamed into opening the window and gingerly extending a dollar. Instead of taking it in one quick motion, he slid it from between her fingers, grazing the side of her hand as he did. In the surprise of being touched, she had a closer look at his sign. It didn't spell *help*. It spelled *hope*.

At home, she scrubbed with soap, but something strange happened. By morning the pain in her neck and back was a dull throb, by lunchtime a twinge, and by dinner a bad memory. She canceled physical therapy for the rest of the month, and no longer needing a pain killer to sleep, broke one in half for relaxation. In strange dreams, she danced with the old man down the center of the boulevard. Years younger, he was handsome and charming, throwing off his cane, exchanging his derby for a top hat, he bent her backwards like Ginger Rogers.

With a mixture of fear and excitement, she looked forward to comparing her dream partner with the real version. Despite a glaring midday sun, he did seem a teeny bit taller and straighter as he shook his sign. Watching from ten cars back, she was glad to see a driver offer water in place of money. Ignoring a blast of horns, she slowed down to miss the light and stopped abruptly beside him. She extended a dollar through the window, testing if his touch had been deliberate and, impossible as it might be, connected to her recovery. Then there it was again. A spark.

This time her glance lingered and she saw that one of his eyes was blue, the other gray, and that his generous nose hung over his lip like an awning. She could imagine a nice mustache and knew he had, once upon a time, been very good-looking, an idea instantly corrected by a smile that didn't apologize for its stained and broken teeth. "I *am* good-looking," that smile said.

She sought him out all summer, her measly dollar waiting in the visor as her car approached, barely aware anymore of the sign he jiggled to catch everyone's attention. She was most aware of the aftereffects of these brief encounters. A period of painlessness and calm that erupted into nocturnal dancing, the old man spinning her along the boulevard, his hand low on her back. The last time she'd seen him was an unplanned trip to the grocery store, the girls in the back, jumping with recognition.

"Our friend, our friend!"

Embarrassed by their excitement, as it seemed to expose her own strange pleasure, she switched routes, and by the start of September was back in therapy, begging the doctor to refill her prescription.

"Mama, Mama!" Summer was shouting, breaking into her reverie.

"We gotta do something," Winter said plainly. The instigator. The plan maker.

She expected they wouldn't let the subject rest. But why this loud when her head hurt? "Stay away, is what you gotta do," she snapped. "They probably on drugs."

She regretted the words the minute they were out of her mouth. At the mention of drugs, the twins got quiet. And sad, their eyes sliding toward their mother's school picture on the shelf. Irene a few years older than their age now. She changed to a gentler tone, but the damage was done.

"Stay away from around there. Okay?"

"Uhu."

"How about you, Winter?"

"Yes, Mama."

The next afternoon the girls were tight-lipped. Mrs. Washington hated when they got like that. Too much quiet made her fret, worse now that the back pain extended into her left leg and foot. After running the washing machine in the morning, she had spent the day on the recliner, trying not to let her gaze drift from the TV to Irene's photo. Over the years the fury had left her eyes and set like clay in the jut of her pimply chin. Seeing the resemblance in the twins, she rummaged her mind for pleasant memories. Finding the old man, she missed the strange balm of his touch and reached into her robe pocket.

She put the TV on mute and got up to fix jelly sandwiches, trying not to make it obvious every step hurt. "You seen Kunta Kinte and his family today?"

Summer opened her mouth, but Winter's leg shot out. Mrs. Washington put on like she was mad and not worried. "When I ask a question, I expect an answer."

"They hiding up behind the dumpster now."

Through her fury, she smiled at Summer. Always the easiest to crack. "You know you ain't supposed to be anywhere near there."

"We needed supplies, Mama. For the project."

She glared at Winter for that bald-faced lie but tried to get more information from Summer before they shut down again. "And what they doing?"

"They worried, Mama."

"And why is that?"

"The boy got a fever."

Winter piped in. "They need help."

"I told you to stay away, didn't I?"

"But they come so far," Summer whined. "And the door gone."

"Door? What you talking about a door?"

Summer gave Winter a quick look. "To the house used to be there."

"Whose house?"

Winter answered in a whisper. "The Underground Railroad, Mama."

Mrs. Washington was beside herself. If her stories weren't coming on, she'd like to drive over to the drugstore and tell the manager.

So he could do what? He always sent his clerks checking around whatever aisle she was at, browsing until her prescription was ready. Every once in a while, like a small apology, the same clerk would be at the checkout and "miss" a couple items.

"You two geniuses do know slavery ended a long time ago."

The girls shot a look between them. "Of course, Mama," Summer said. "But . . ."

She decided to call their bluff with a threat. "I have a good mind to call the police."

"You can't!"

She shot Winter a warning look. "I don't want to, but you gotta think of them children."

"The baby's sick bad."

Mrs. Washington paused from emptying the washing machine. This new development, plus the extra tab she'd taken, made her forget to yell at them.

"Oh Lord! So, what they gonna do?"

"They don't know. They asking us."

"They scared they gonna get caught and sent back down to Mississippi and get beat and separated."

Mrs. Washington snapped a wet dish towel and tossed it into the dryer. "Mississippi?" It was the one thing she could make sense of for she had people down there she'd lost touch with. Poor as church mice, last she heard. Or doing better than her. Depended on who you talked to. She took a deep breath. Maybe she could reason the girls out of their foolishness.

"When these people supposed to have left Mississippi?"

The girls kept opening and shutting their mouths like on that game show "To Tell the Truth." Finally, Winter spoke in a voice too serious for an eleven-year-old.

"More than a hundred years ago, Mama . . . can you believe that? They say they been ducking and dodging and they got here by the skin of they teeth and can't go no farther."

Mrs. Washington glanced at the table where more library books had been added to the pile. Then she got mad. Doggone that Gifted Program. Making her girls into a couple of white kids like in those Harry Potter books they read over and over. For Halloween they were twin wizards and before that something called a Bilbo Baggins and a Frodo. She was embarrassed taking them trick-or-treating, but luckily everyone thought they were hobos in their raggedy clothes.

She held her breath for the count of ten, then let it out slow. This year for the Famous People Project, Winter was preparing to be Toni Morrison and Summer, Bessie Coleman. Like their mother, they were doing the best they could crossing that long bridge back and forth to school every day. No deep dark water, no nightmare Tallahatchie, but a child could drown just the same. She had to be patient if she didn't want to lose them.

"Did you tell them slavery ended?"

"Of course, we did, Mama. Then we said America ain't safe for Black people."

"Why you tell them that?"

"That's what you say, Mama."

That was true. She had been warning them since they were babies.

"They asked about Canada. Which way and how far. But Winter told them the rest of what you say."

"What's that?"

"'Nowhere in the world is safe for Black people.'"

Mrs. Washington's body ached from listening and when they finished, staring at her with those round dark eyes like she might actually believe their story, she almost started laughing. Over a hundred years on the run? She wondered if the people had really said this or if the girls had made it up.

There was a long pause as the clock in the kitchen tried to make rhyme and reason. Time, Mrs. Washington thought to herself. Heals all wounds. Second chances. Don't push. She decided to wait until after supper to talk some more. By then, their heads were buried in home-work, so she took herself a tablet and let the subject drop. In the morning, seeing their backpacks loaded down like hikers going up Mt. Everest, she hoped they'd lost interest.

"We gotta work on our project after school," Summer announced.

"'If you free, you need to free somebody else.'"

"What's that you mumbling, Winter?"

"Something I heard."

"Hmph." It sounded dangerous to Mrs. Washington, so she nipped it in the bud. "I hear about you hanging around those people, I'll whup both your behinds."

She had dozed longer than usual. They were late, so she called the school.

"Nothing I heard about going on," the secretary said. "The Famous People Project is always at the *end* of the year."

She sounded snotty, like everybody was supposed to remember that, and Mrs. Washington had a good mind to go down there and slap her upside the head.

Shaking with cold that comes with worry, she pulled on her wig and crawled to the pharmacy because the car wouldn't start. More than half-way there she realized the temperature had fallen. When had the season changed, she wondered, and wished she'd worn a jacket. There was the rusty dumpster the girls mentioned, on the patchy lawn out back, but no sign of anyone. She went inside and talked to the clerk at the checkout, a willowy girl who looked like someone who'd grown up on Mulberry Street.

"Thought I was seeing double," the girl said with a laugh, then cutting her eyes at the manager, lowered her voice. "They asked me to help a family with sick kids."

"That's them," Mrs. Washington said. "What did you do?"

"Gave them some water. Haven't seen your twins since."

She stood outside the front of the store, peering up and down the side-walk, her heart racing and the cold in her belly turned to ice. Could the girls, worried about the whuppin she'd never give, taken another way home and gotten lost? Or had she misunderstood about the project? Maybe they were at a classmate's house. They'd done that before. Crossed over into the neighborhood where they went trick-or-treating. Unless they met up at the library. She tried to remember if any books were still piled on the coffee table.

A teenager walked around her into the store, his shoulders reared back and his narrow hips barely holding up his jeans. Whether he was going to pocket condoms or pick up his Grandma's prescription, or both, he was somebody who wouldn't take the manager's shit without cussing.

Condoms! Could they be running behind boys already? Winter, maybe.

She took a deep breath, telling herself she was getting worked up for nothing. Surely, they were home now and seeing the car in the yard, wondering where she was. Summer would be scared. Both would be worried and hungry. She almost ran back into the store to pick up a box of macaroni and cheese, then deciding it would arouse suspicion, went around back one more time. *Check behind the dumpster*, a voice said from the back of her head. *To set your mind at ease.* And way deep down, *To see they ain't raped and strangled.*

There was a man a few yards away, the shadow of an oak tree spread over him. She figured he was waiting for her to leave so he could scrounge for returnables, but he stepped forward, his hands empty except for a cane. It was the man from the intersection in a baseball cap and a clean jacket. An ordinary man. She flushed with embarrassment.

"They gone."

"Huh?" He couldn't possibly know why she was here.

"Them folks your girls talking about."

Embarrassment turned to fear and anger. The man was an imposter. She squared her feet. "What you got to do with my kids?"

He ignored the insinuation and came closer so she could see his blue and gray eyes. Probing.

"I don't know if you've ever seen salmon swimming upstream, but that's what I thought of looking at the commotion on the boulevard. Two little fishies fighting the current to tell me about some lost folks up behind here."

Seized by panic, she lunged forward, prepared to drag him to the police herself, answer for what happened to her girls, but as she did, he raised a hand. Just that. Like a parent warning a child not to cross a line. Under the spell of his hand, her feet, fist, and lips were frozen.

"I walked them home," he said. "And explained that folks take this long to get here got plenty of what they need squirreled up." He paused a moment, reminding her of those weeks she went out of the way to give him a dollar, before adding, "Hope."

Hope? She hadn't paid his sign any mind. It was a prop, like his cane. The sorts of things panhandlers used up and down the boulevard. Each one a little different to catch the eye. She willed words that wouldn't come, and unable to move, wished every torture and horror to fall on his head.

"I told them in the absence of everything else, hope is a filling bread, a quenching drink. That an ounce of hope get you to the next stop."

He waited again as questions ran through her mind. Was he suggesting that hope lifted her pain? That you could buy it for a dollar or a plastic water bottle? She shook the ideas off as impossible and glanced at his cane. The steep trip up from the boulevard to Mulberry Street was difficult. Then the several more blocks here. Except he didn't sound winded. She suspected he was like her deceased husband, hiding unexpected strength and cunning behind the cane. A fraud. A thief, stealing the words out of her mouth.

"You want to guess what them girls did next?"

Now a scream stuck halfway up her throat. *He's seen your girls. Been to your house.*

"They cried like angels."

Her eyes stuck in their sockets, she tried to burn holes into his face.

"When I asked why, they said because the people ain't had no hope. 'We stole it,' the tall one said.

Her Winter!

"Stole hope?" I said. "How do two sweet fishies steal hope when a whole government and its police force can't do it? And they say, 'We told them America ain't safe for Black people. That nowhere safe in the whole wide world.'"

She groaned like a gag was tied around her mouth, furious he could recite her words with a bitterness that came across as downright mean. A bitterness she was sure she hadn't used.

"Now I don't entirely disagree with you, Madam. But you black enough to know ain't no safe place unless we offer it."

He was keeping a close eye on her as he spoke. The same game Mr. Washington used to play. Accuse her of terrible things, like driving Irene away, when it was the other way around. A protest gurgled in her throat but went no farther. Given a chance, she'd have liked to kill him with her bare hands. He shook a finger in her face.

"I gave *you* hope, so why you ain't shared it?"

The words shot unexpected from her mouth. "Slaves! They told my girls they were runaways!"

She waited for the ridiculous story to sink into his dumb head so he could understand she was no fool to be trifled with. Not anymore. Not like how she'd done Irene. This time she would go down fighting for her babies. She would . . .

As if reading her intentions, he stepped back, but it was she who cowered because he had begun to grow. Taller and taller, throwing the hat, tossing away his cane, his head of hair, white as a cloud, disappearing into the sky.

She ran for home, hobbling, trying not to be seen, crying, as she was, and cold.

Going to see about her girls.

COLOREDMAGIC

Ten years after The Fire, residents compensated after a long legal battle, the neighborhood was rebuilt. A mere month after the ribbon cutting and the mayor making overly much of his role in reparations, everyone found the same flyer in their mailbox. There was a before and after photo of a woman. In the first her facial skin was melted down to white. In the second, she was a flawless shade of milk chocolate.

Burned and suffering unsightly white and pink spots?

When cocoa butter alone isn't enough,
We got you!

Rebrown with ColoredMagic*!*

Towelettes that respond to
your individual body chemistry
to restore the perfect shade.

Not a cover . . . like makeup,
but a Second Coming.

Fair, Medium, Ethiopian—
we got you!

Let the rebrowning *begin!*

ColoredMagic*!*

Call 315-555-0199. Serious inquiries only.

London was surprised when someone actually called. "Told you so," said his pal Jacklyn, who was the woman in the flyer. She worked in a costume shop that sprang up every October. "There's a sucker born every minute."

"You just make that up?"

"Naw. P.T. Barnum. Greatest showman ever lived."

London knocked on Miss Carter's door the next day. An hour late. Miss Carter rolled her lips at his worn-down shoes.

"Where your car?"

The truth: He'd tried to borrow Jacklyn's car to look more professional, but she was pissed about the last time.

The lie: "I apologize. I was up the other end of the street seeing other clients along the way. And you know how some of us can talk."

"I'm not used to waiting," the lady snapped, but he noticed her left eyebrow go up when he said "clients." He also noticed the extra layer of makeup caked in the wrinkles of her forehead. He had forgotten that old people like his Aunt Pat, who nobody took to the Family Buffet anymore, expected to be first all the time.

"Let me show you something."

He clicked the video of Jacklyn on his phone and gave it to Miss Carter. Three times she handed it back in her white gloves and asked to watch Jacklyn do it again: wipe white makeup off her face with a towelette. As the paper crossed her mouth, her expression changing from sad to a pouty sex kitten, the lower half of her face became a medium shade of brown. By the time she finished wiping off the rest of the white, London had to fight his nature. Jacklyn was that good.

After the video, he showed Miss Carter a picture of the re-labelled container from the Dollar Store, zooming in on the fake ingredients. Cocoa butter was highlighted, along with the reference to a Second Coming.

"You sure that's not overdoing it?" he'd asked a week ago.

Jacklyn looked at him like he'd fallen off a turnip truck. "You know we eat this stuff up."

Miss Carter had her pocketbook on her lap taking out a checkbook when she got cold feet. Or maybe running her own game. London wasn't sure. It was right after he said, "Once you pay me and I process the order, it will arrive by mail in three to five business days." She pursed her cracked lips so hard a deep trench opened below her nose, and she held the checkbook shut.

"You have any samples? You know, like the Avon lady?"

"Well, I normally do," he lied. "But *ColoredMagic* is selling like hotcakes. Everybody trying to rebrown before summer. I ran out at the last house."

The thought of anyone browning before her didn't go over well with Miss Carter. This time when she frowned, a white number seven flashed between her penciled eyebrows. He was sure there wasn't a single real hair in those eyebrows and imagined how she must have run from the flames, covering her nose and mouth with a wet towel. Like the other houses he'd visited on Mulberry Street there were no old photos on the walls. No way of seeing Miss Carter from back in the day.

"I'll be straight with you. The results in the video have been speeded up. The process takes a few weeks to complete."

"How many?"

"Two tops. Ten to fourteen days. Everyone is different." He wondered what she looked like without makeup or the curly brown wig she kept pulling down. He wondered if she was burned bald, then forced himself to smile (Jacklyn's coaching) until she smiled back. She uncapped a pen but still didn't open the checkbook.

"And what if it doesn't work?"

"Money back guarantee. As head of the company, and nephew of Cap Biggs—"

She drew in a sharp breath. "That's right. Cap Biggs is one of your people."

"He sure is, ma'am."

"We used to hang out in the same circle. How he doing?"

Uncle Cap had had to crawl out of his collapsed bedroom and was burned on the chest, neck, and chin. Would go to his grave disfigured and in pain. That's why London pulled up a picture taken a year before that awful day. It was one of Uncle Cap at the Baseball Hall of Fame. He liked to brag that he missed a shot at the big league. London almost burst out laughing to see Miss Carter sweating over the old man. Uncle Cap was a red-brown complexion that glowed in the sun when he stood on the mound. The color of a legend.

"That's him. Living down in New York. No clubbing anymore but a Big Yankees fan."

"But I heard . . . " Her old face was reliving the painful memories of fire and extensive hospitalization. Not many on the street were untouched by the flames or the embers.

London puffed out his chest. "My first client."

She examined the image a full minute, until London offered to call Uncle Cap for an endorsement. "Probably napping, but he won't mind."

"No, no, no!" Miss Carter tittered. London figured she wouldn't want that, talking about skin care with a former suitor. Let alone talk about being scarred. "I guess this stuff really do work."

Five days later, when nothing came in the mail, Miss Carter tried calling London. She tried every day, a few times a day, but no one picked up, and she couldn't leave a message because the box was full. In the mean-time, Marjorie from church called about the cruise she was organizing. Miss Carter, who had once been a popular ringleader of the electric slide, said, "I'm thinking about it."

Actually, it was all she'd been thinking about. A framed photo of herself at The Captain's Ball to replace the one that had burned to ash. An album of photos and a different outfit on every page. But while wraps and wigs and a straw hat were always stylish aboard ship, and she was a whiz at makeup, what if she met a nice gentleman? She wasn't too old for that, was she? She would rather die sad and lonely than have her scalp come uncovered in the middle of intimacies.

"You still using that cocoa butter cream I brought you?" Marjorie asked in a tone that had too much pity for Miss Carter's liking. The jar had long been replaced by others with the same disappointing results.

"I need a week to decide," she snapped. What she needed was the rebrowning ointment. She steeled herself for the prayer she expected to follow.

"I'll give you three days," Marjorie said without an ounce of warmth. "And then I need your deposit."

She was waiting on the mail carrier when she saw Cap's son, the one who was a teacher up at the high school, leaving Pat's house across the street. Same tall build with thick biceps under his T-shirt. A type of man built for baseball. Beautiful honey-colored complexion like his mother, God rest her soul. He was away at college during The Fire.

She had on her sunglasses, a wide brimmed hat pulled low on her forehead, and white gloves when she called him over.

"How you doing up at the school?" she started in, going from there into a dozen questions before getting to the point. "I been trying to reach London." She pretended not to notice him wince. "You know how to contact him?"

Gary had just an hour ago bought some weed from his cousin. "Can't say I do," he lied. No way was he going to be an intermediary between

London and anybody. These old Mulberry Street people were bad enough. Things got complicated with London.

"Well, if you see him, tell him he's got something I need."

Gary nodded, unable to lie again out loud. He hadn't figured Miss Carter for self-medicating, but she wouldn't be the first surprise on this street. Folks had these beautiful rebuilt houses, a well-paved street, and healthy trees. Things looked fine on the outside, but he heard stories about people wasting the settlement money. Losing heavy at the casino, drinking themselves into a stupor every night, drugs. A suicide too, although they didn't call it that. They were depressed. They made him depressed.

He made a move to go, but she had him by the arm. He glanced at the white glove against his brown skin and felt guilty, like he always did, if he stayed too long on Mulberry Street.

"How your father doing in New York?" she said. "Still moving with the high rollers?"

"He's fine, ma'am. Looking good, last time I saw him."

Lie, lie, lie. His father had met a woman online who told him about a radical skin treatment. He claimed to be seeing results every day, but a fool could hear the desperation in his voice. Gary hadn't been home to save him from The Fire, so when the next disaster came, when the woman spent up all his money and left him high and dry, he would go down there and bring him home.

"Tell me honest. Is the treatment working?"

So, she'd heard about it too. Gary looked down at the little woman squeezing his arm and decided he would pass her message on to London after all. But as for the quack treatment that stole his father's money, he wouldn't send his worst enemy down that rabbit hole. He would save her.

"Miss Carter, if my father was here, he'd tell you himself. Best treatment is cocoa butter and Jesus. You gotta keep the faith."

He was surprised how his words seemed to rouse her. She practically flew up the porch stairs and back into her house.

A BENCH ON THE MOON

Private apartment in Victorian house near lake, sleeps 2-4. Separate
entrance with security code. Kitchenette.
Private bath.
Soundproof.

The sisters turned from the house to each other. There was a woman
hanging clothes across the street. She didn't hide the fact she was staring.

"Better be no trouble," Linda, the older one, said softly. She'd seen
plenty of YouTube videos where it wasn't safe for Black people to stay in
an Airbnb.

They lifted the bags out of the trunk, then helped Mama from the
back seat. Blinking at the late afternoon sun, she locked her arms at her
side and flapped her hands like flippers.

"You get Mama," Midge said, restraining an urge to dust her off. "I'll
take care of the bags."

Linda nodded. Her nerves were shot from the long ride and the sooner Mama was settled, the better. Midge, as impulsive as ever, had booked
the two-night stay, and, despite her misgivings, Linda was going to make
the best of it. They had agreed to take turns having a walk on the beach,
shopping, and reading a book. Entering the pretty New England town,
they glimpsed the possibilities, then saw those possibilities flicker.

Mama had been good. They left home on time, stopped for coffee
to go, and she had seemed pleased with the outing. She said so herself a
number of times. "I'm being good," as she sipped coffee that had surely

gotten cold. "I'm being good," as she nibbled cheese crackers Linda passed from the front seat, ignoring Midge's second reminder that the car was a rental. She even contributed to the conversation when Midge brought up the decrepit state of Mulberry Street.

"If they can put a man on the moon, you think they could fix the potholes and cracks. Half the streetlights don't come on."

Mama leaned forward and tugged Linda's arm. "You remember us watching on the couch?"

Midge was completely lost. As she was discovering, Linda and Mama, both skinny and dressing younger than their ages, intuitively understood each other. Midge went to college on the other side of the country, settled into a comfortable weight, and rarely visited, while Linda lived in a suburb and stopped by Mulberry Street on her way to and from work.

"I sure do. I wanted to be the first Black astronaut."

Midge had missed the iconic moment by five years, during which six other missions succeeded. She glanced from the road to her sister. "Why you think we never went back?"

"*I* know," Mama said.

They glanced at each other. Mama was listening. Interested. They used to talk all the time. Loud discussions—sometimes arguments—about everything under the sun. Politics, Hollywood, gay rights, police brutality. Even religion wasn't a settled subject.

"And why is that?" Linda asked, eager to keep the conversation going.

"There's nowhere to sit."

"Come again, Mama?" Midge tried to catch her eye in the rearview mirror, but Mama's eyes were everywhere and nowhere.

"I said, there's nowhere to sit on the moon."

There was an awkward silence as that sunk in. Even Linda had no reply. She'd been hinting over the phone that Mama wasn't making sense lately, but she could never remember a solid example. Now she didn't have to.

Mama went back to crunching crackers, leaving orange crumbs on the seat and floor. She didn't take any interest in the sites they passed. Not even in the twinkling lake on the approach to the apartment.

"Look! Look!" cried Linda, snapping a photo with her phone.

"Water," Mama said blandly. "I could have stayed home and seen water."

During the planning stages, the sisters talked about a picnic lunch on the beach, but Mama's indifference stifled their enthusiasm. Inside the cozy apartment, they pulled an extra chair over to the café table and tucked into rotisserie chicken, potato salad, a fresh baguette, and wine, with iced tea for Mama.

"You two eat like pigs."

The sisters tapped glasses of chardonnay and ignored the barb. It was not much different than the things Mama used to say. Mooing like a cow if they drank milk, even nicknaming Rosemary "Midge" just as she hit puberty.

"A smidgen of this, smidgen of that—how you plan to go to college if you too big to get out the front door?"

Midge cleaned her plate with the last chunk of bread and popped it in her mouth, remembering why she hadn't visited in over a year. Not since Uncle Jackie's funeral.

Her ex-husband had also been obsessed with weight and critical of her yo-yo diets. "Your problem is you can't stand success, Rosemary," he used to say. She gave up on marriage and counting calories the same year she met her girlfriend, Maura.

She nodded gratefully at Linda for topping off her glass and decided if they spent the weekend indoors, getting drunk-faced like her students, she'd be fine with that. When Mama stood up, using the table for leverage, Midge took mean pleasure in the beginning of a stoop in her mother's back. Since her late seventies, Mama had steadily lost the toned body she used to show off in her stylish clothes. She was eighty-five.

"I'm ready to go home," she said now. "It's starting to get dark and I want to go to bed."

Midge rolled the wine like a sommelier. It was seven o'clock. "We're staying the night, Mama."

Mama blinked like she'd done earlier by the car. "I want to go home. It's dark and I'm tired."

"How about some television?" Linda said, stacking the dishes. "We can put on our pajamas and make a little party?"

"Are you stupid?" Mama snapped. "Grown women having a pajama party?"

Midge winked at Linda who looked on the verge of tears. "Maybe it is time we turned in." She yawned dramatically to make the point.

There were two beds in the unit. A pull-out sofa for Mama and a queen which they'd planned to share. Mama would fall asleep quickly after the three-hour drive, and they would whisper and giggle like girls. There was another bottle of wine in the cooler. They would stream a movie. The point of the trip was to be together. Fun.

They were propped up, messaging back home, when she shouted for them to stop.

"We're—"

"—I said stop and get over here!"

"We're sleeping in the big bed, Mama."

"Get over here!"

Linda took the pillow and got into bed with Mama.

"You too!" Mama told Midge.

"There's no room, Mama."

"You too!"

They lay in that tight space for an hour. Waiting for Mama to fall asleep. Midge on the outside, feeling the hardness of the couch frame along her left side, managed to pop in earbuds and turn on her phone. From the moment the screen lit up, she was pulled away from Mama and the uncomfortable bed into Maura's chatter about just getting off work, heading to meet up a group of mutual friends at a bar. She felt Linda adjust her position in the middle. Snuggling.

"Turn that off!"

"What, Mama?"

"I said turn off that goddamn thing and go to sleep."

A light flew across the shades, casting shadows of the bushes outside, shadows that crept across the ceiling and wavered before it was dark again. Mama sat up. "What the hell is going on?"

"It's a car," Linda said.

"Shut up. I didn't ask you."

Midge felt Linda's body stiffen and took over. "She's right, Mama. We're on a main street."

"I want to go home."

"It's too late."

"What's that noise?"

Linda kept her head down, but Midge pulled herself up to hear what Mama was hearing. There was a low whistle of air coming from the floor grate on Mama's side. Mama stood up, shivering in the narrow space between the window and the bed, her nightgown flying up around her knees as she pat- patted the edges of the paper shade. When another car passed, the distress on her face was enough to break Midge's heart, reminding her of the day Mama told them about Papa. The great-grand-father who sent oranges and grapefruit in crates and crisp five-dollar bills for their birthdays was dying, and Mama said she would be gone a week. She came home a month later, still crying.

"Get me a board."

Midge wondered if she was going to cry now. "Why do you need a board?"

"Get me the goddamn board."

Midge let Linda keep pretending to sleep and searched for a board or something like one. The makeshift shelving in the closet hadn't been permanently nailed, so she brought that. Mama placed it over the grate and got back in bed. When Midge did the same, Linda, reaching over her hip, took her hand and squeezed it. There was an entire conversation in the gesture. Thank you. Remember. I took a whuppin for your little behind a few times. Let's sleep. We'll get up early, walk the beach, read, visit the shops, waste money on souvenirs, and then, cross our fingers, take pictures on that famous bench.

Coming through the town, Mama had complained of being thirsty, so they stopped beside a park to get water from the trunk.

"May as well get out," Midge said. "Stretch our legs."

Linda caught her enthusiasm. "Come on, Mama, We're on vacation."

Mama had balked but complied, and as they approached the bench, Midge made the discovery.

"Look! It's a 'bench by the road.'"

"A what?" said her sister.

"See there. A plaque about Toni Morrison."

Linda tried to read it, but Mama plopped herself, deliberately it seemed, right in front. "Can you slide over?" she said. "I want to read about Toni Morrison."

"Who's that?" Mama snapped.

"A Black writer," Midge said. "She inspired the project." Then she proceeded to tell them how the bench was meant to give space to unspoken and forgotten African Americans' stories. The stories of formerly enslaved people.

"That's beautiful," Linda said. "Mama, let me take a picture of you and—"

"—and what? A stupid nigger?"

"Mama!" Not for the first time, Midge imagined striking her mother in the face. This moment felt the closest.

"I'll say it again. A stupid nigger!"

A white woman, strolling toward the bus stop, looked up from her phone before hurrying along.

"Let's go," Linda whispered to Midge. "Just go to the apartment." But Midge, always Midge, couldn't let it rest.

"We don't use that word, Mama."

Mama sucked her teeth at the white woman's back and spoke louder. "That's what they call us, isn't it? *Nigger*!"

After an hour, it seemed as though Mama was asleep. Linda too, her hand loosening its hold but her arm draping Midge's side like a tight belt. Unable to move without waking Mama, enduring the pinch of the bed frame digging into her left shoulder, Midge sweat so that the little moles between her breasts began to itch. It was unbearable, and she wondered why she'd bothered to return East. Early in the planning, Linda had hinted that a road trip with Mama was a bad idea, but she hadn't been specific. That business at the bench and now this—Midge felt tricked by both of them and decided she would drive home in the morning, tonight in the dark if it came to it. She would offer to reimburse Linda for the rental, knowing Linda would refuse, and then she would call the airline and book an earlier flight back to Maura.

Marjorie stared out the car window. She had taken as much as she could from two women she didn't know babbling about another woman she didn't know telling stories. Like that was something special. Dumb bitches. She knew how to tell stories and there was nothing special about it. A story was something you repeated and not things you made up as you went along. That's why books bored her. Liars wrote books. Marjorie's stories adhered to what Papa called "An honest reckoning." Details mattered.

In her lucid moments, she realized she was forgetting details. But which ones and how many? She didn't know. There were gaps confirmed by these women's faces. That's why she stopped telling stories like she used to. Why she was angry a lot of the time. Her stories about living down South and coming North, her stories about family scattered from citizen to circumference, were in pieces that didn't fit together anymore.

Like leaving the house. Which house? Which morning? One of the women cried out "Look! Look!" but Mama said, "Don't open the shade, Nell!" She'd been warning about that shade since they sat down on the train. And of course Marjorie, who they called Nell, didn't listen.

"I was always a snoop," she used to say as a preamble to telling a story. "I listened through the wall. I watched through the keyhole."

The sisters startled from sleep. Mama, now standing over their heads, squeezed into the narrow space behind the pull-out sofa, was shouting at the window that faced the front of the house. Where the car was parked. Where the neighbor had watched them while she pinned little dresses and beach clothes to the line.

"Troll! Baby killer! Motherfucker!"

"Mama, don't talk like that," Linda pleaded.

Midge, listening to the two going back and forth, felt nothing but disgust. It had to stop. "People can hear you, Mama. They'll call the police."

Mama leaned over them with her fists balled and her lips tight. "Let 'em try."

"Shhh, Mama," Linda said.

"I'll shush you, you stupid bitch."

Midge felt her sister's body deflate like a rubber toy and sat up, breaking the chain of their clasped hands and spoke to her mother like she was a bad child. "That's enough. Get in bed."

It seemed to do the trick, except now Linda was crying.

"I gotta pee," Mama said.

There were white people outside, pointing and laughing like she was in the zoo instead of wearing her Sunday best. And Mama shouting, "What

I tell you? What I tell you?" as the train picked up speed, but not fast enough for Nell not to see the tree along the tracks.

"What's that, Mama? What's that hanging off the tree?"

She had only remembered the train ride lately, the memory unearthed with Linda's fussing about Midge coming and the three of them taking a little trip. That's what Mama had said too.

"Stop that crying, Nell. Me, you, and Jackie taking a little trip is all."

That was a lie for Jackie, who was just stupid enough to believe it.

Side-by-side on the edge of the bed, Midge and Linda listened to the toilet dispenser spinning. Midge stood up. She stared at the coffee and tea island, the café table where they'd had their dinner, a third chair pulled up from the writing desk. Their suitcases were lined up by the door. Ready to go home. It was 3 a.m.

"You don't think there's a camera in here, do you?" Linda asked.

"People get in trouble for doing that."

"But they do it, don't they? Don't they stream it on the internet?"

Something fell over in the bathroom and Midge went to the locked door. "Are you okay, Mama?"

"Go away, bitch."

Marjorie wet down the toilet paper to make it stick to the glass, but it kept sliding down. Letting the faces in.

They wouldn't have left, wouldn't have been on that stupid train at all if it hadn't been for Jackie and Buss Ward. The dog was as dumb as Jackie. A beagle mix that was supposed to keep them safe when they went along the path to Papa's house but had his mind on squirrels and chipmunks.

"You come across crackers hunting our property, you don't say nothing," she heard every day for as far back as she could think. "Stay on the path and keep a hold on your baby brother."

What was she supposed to do when Buss Ward took off and Jackie went running behind?

Four a.m. Mama seemed asleep, but the sisters weren't taking any chances. At five, Midge texted the owner: "Leaving early due to family emergency." She didn't expect a refund but a little sympathy would feel good. And if there was a tape of the abuse they'd endured, she decided she would welcome it to prove how hard they had tried to be good. She quietly put the board back in the closet, picked clots of wet toilet paper off the bathroom window and from behind the commode, and used a hairpin to remove the rolled tubes of paper from the air duct. If Mama was this crazy, maybe she needed to be in a home.

She had dozed off, the car keys in her hand, when Mama sat up and said she wouldn't leave without makeup and her hair done. It was 8:00. But after Linda's hard work making her thin, gray tufts into something like a bouffant, she demanded the cap right off Midge's head. In her cotton slacks and Cal State T-shirt, she looked ten years younger under the brim.

"Why we can't stay?" she whined as she took slow sips of coffee. "Why we got to leave?" as they urged her out of the room and down the steps of the house.

A woman at the corner stopped to stick her head inside a baby carriage, while a toddler ran ahead, waving at them. Midge watched Mama for signs of shouting a profanity, but she only smiled and waved back. Inside the car, she plucked at the cap and sulked.

Nell was on Papa's lap, hugging him like she'd never let go, while Jackie sat on the floor with his lips pooched out. Papa called her his favorite no matter whose feelings he hurt.

Of course, she was the favorite. She was the first grandchild and the one and only for three whole years. And Papa talked to her about any-thing she asked and didn't hush her like she was a dumbbell. A question was rattling in her head, mainly because she'd never asked it before and it seemed like she should have.

"Was you a slave, Papa?"

He took a pipe from his mouth and squinted. "I'm old, but I ain't that old!"

"Was your Mama and Papa slaves?"

This time, he threw back his gray head and laughed like the question tickled his funny bone.

"Whoa, Nelly! Who told you that? They was just babies when slavery ended. Babies." He pointed his chin at Jackie, still sulking after his dog, Buss Ward. "Not much bigger than that runt over there."

Papa. He had an answer for anything she wanted to know, but not for what she asked next.

"Why we got to leave you?"

Midge drove slowly through the streets. The kitschy shops were open-ing, rolling their wares onto the sidewalk. There were already tourists buying pocketbooks and scarfs and T-shirts. When they approached the souvenir shop opposite the Toni Morrison bench, Linda sighed. The day before she had mentioned wanting magnets for her co-workers and a mug for the neighbor watching out for Mama's house. She turned with surprise when Midge pulled into an open spot. Midge bit her lip as if to say, "Do we take the chance?"

Linda's husband wasn't crazy about the idea of Mama moving in with them, but he wasn't going to say no either. "What will she do all day?" he grumbled, so she brought Mama to the senior center to test it out. The tour had gone well, the director being a pleasant white woman.

Their kids had gone to school together. She showed them the rooms for exercise classes and crafts.

"Hello everyone," Miss Bridget announced to the dozen or so ladies at the work benches. "Marjorie is going to join us. Isn't that wonderful?"

There were polite smiles from the women making birdhouses. As they were leaving, a woman, knitting needles poking out of a sack on her lap, was wheeling herself in. Mama was still knitting then and, like nowadays, could be charming, except when she wasn't. She extended a greeting, but the woman didn't reply. Linda saw the hearing aid in her ear and assumed the woman hadn't heard, but Mama turned quiet and was almost curt when Miss Bridget escorted them to the door with the program schedule and said cheerily, "Hope to see you back soon." Mama managed a tight smile and said, "Of course," but once in the car, as Midge later told her husband, she exploded.

"I should have turned the goddamned wheelchair over."

"What happened? What is it?"

"The bitch gave me the stink eye."

"The old lady? She had a hearing problem."

Mama gave her a hard stare. "She had a nigger problem is what she had."

"Oh, Mama, please don't."

Teddy thought it was funny, said Marjorie was a smart old lady, but Linda never again broached the subject of Mama moving in and he didn't ask.

Linda picked her purse from the floor. "Let's go into the shop, Mama. Just a quick stop."

"I don't want any damn junk."

"Mama."

"Go, if you want. I'll stay right here."

The sisters stared at each other, speaking in the silent language of siblings. They would keep an eye through the shop window and only browse for five minutes instead of ten. The car was in the shade, the windows were cracked, and Mama had plenty of water. Midge made sure the child safety locks were on and they headed in with a couple backward glances.

"Fuckers," Marjorie muttered. She opened her purse and checked the hidden compartment, counting out the bills, no matter the denomination, as $10, $20, $50 . . . $100. Then she checked her pocket for change.

She noticed a man reading a newspaper on a bench across the street. He folded it up and walked toward a crowd of people waiting at a bus stop. She sneered at the bench. Something, she couldn't remember, she disliked about it. When her door wouldn't open, she wiggled between the front seats and slipped out the driver's side, ignoring the honking as she crossed the street in time to get on the bus.

"Whoa, Nelly," the driver said. "That's more than enough money."

She rode a long time. Watching commuters get on and off, clutching her purse to her lap. She waited until the streets began to crack and the cracks lead from rundown to ruined. Things were beginning to feel familiar. The bus windows were open. Mixed with the bus fumes were fried breakfast smells that made her stomach growl. This was better. When she saw some of her neighbors in front of a laundromat, she pulled the cord over her head.

"You know where you're going?" the driver asked kindly.

"Oh, yes," she said, so cheered by seeing familiar faces she forgot and smiled at him. For where her neighbors were, Mulberry Street couldn't be far. But as the bus pulled away, they disappeared.

She checked inside the laundromat and the Dollar Store next to it, then inside a thrift shop and a bakery where she bought herself a couple rolls. She was jostled by kids in bathing suits and gave a homeless man the rolls. Wondering what to do next, she heard singing and followed it down a side street and into a building with a giant silver moon hanging above the door. The singing was coming from inside.

It took a moment for her eyes to adjust. There was a man sipping at the far end of a bar and two women arguing at a window table. But softly. Behind the bar, a man in a white apron looked up with surprise, then smiled. For a second he was her brother, then her husband, then nobody she knew. That was better. The music was nice and there was a cool breeze from somewhere. She slid onto a stool, still clutching her purse.

"What will it be, Miss?"

She glanced from side to side, trying to remember what she liked to drink. The man at the end of the bar was rocking to the music, his eyes closed and his glass too far away to see.

"Vodka," she said finally.

The bartender's eyes got large. "You want that with tonic?"

She thought there had been something bitter and red about the drink. Something that suited her mood watching the young people crowd the dance floor at a wedding. No room for an old lady like her. Forgotten except for a drink.

"Juice," she said. "Kind of sour." She smiled. He had pretty brown eyes.

The bartender slapped the counter. "Cape Cod. Ladies love it."

"Six now," he said a few minutes later, setting down the glass. "Unless you want to start a tab." He said it like a joke. Was he joking? Whatever it meant, she decided she liked it and nodded. It sounded like it meant not opening her purse.

"What is this place?" she asked.

"*The Silvery Moon.* My father opened it in 1969, same summer the song came out."

Song? She sipped slowly, noticing the dark TV screen above the mirrored shelves of liquor. Where was the music coming from? When the bartender put down a bowl of peanuts, she tuned out the singer and hoped she wasn't making a pig of herself.

"So, what's your story?" he asked.

She liked the way he looked her in the eye when he spoke.

"Lot of stories," she quipped. "But you'll need boots and an airplane." He looked confused for a moment, an idiot, and she thought of those two women who disappeared. She was glad to be rid of them. They were jealous of her and wanted the money.

She watched him move away, wiping down the counter, while the man at the far end got up and ambled to the stool beside her. He wore a coat that had long ago been nicely tailored, and he needed a shave, and Marjorie wondered how those scratchy hairs would feel on her cheeks. Dancing. She leaned into the sweet cigarette smells around him and heard him crooning.

"What's that all about?" she asked.

"Love me some Jackie," the man said.

"You know Jackie?"

"Of course, I do." He cocked his head toward the bartender and chuckled. "Plays Mr. Excitement nonstop on Tuesdays to bring in the crowd. Now tell me about the boots and an airplane."

"Huh?" She shook herself from a sudden image of a little boy crying for his dog. Maybe this man could help find him, find both of them. He reached in front of her and took a handful of peanuts— her peanuts— but he interrupted before she could protest.

"You said you had a story but Stanley over there would need boots and an airplane to hear it. I want to know why."

The bartender hurried back over. "It's okay," he told the man. "If that's what the lady says, that's what she says."

Marjorie turned around at the sound of laughter. Two women by the window, one covering her mouth, returned nosy glances in her direction. "Bitches," she thought. Jealous that the men were talking to her. The bartender had disappeared, but the scruffy man was smiling like he had all the time in the world. She put her purse on the counter and wove her fingers into a bridge to hide the moles on her neck.

"Say again?" she asked the man.

"The boots and the airplane," he repeated patiently. "You said you had a story but Stanley would need boots and an airplane to hear it. I'm curious what you meant by that."

Marjorie rocked with a full, youthful laugh and her skin flushed thinking he might ask her to dance. But then she remembered Jackie, sitting on her lap and crying for that damn dog, and she pulled her feet up a rung, hunched with her face hidden until he disappeared.

"Marooned," the bartender told his partner later. "Like she'd ridden the bar stool across the galaxy and crash landed on the moon."

"Holy," the scruffy man told his sponsor. "Someone to make you denounce the Devil and turn back to God."

The women clasped hands above the table, their heads nearly touching. Whatever they were saying, it was between them. There was a resemblance in the dark shade of their skin, but only a fool would think they were sisters.

Lifting her face at last, acknowledging the men with a nod, aware of the interested silence from the table, Marjorie realized she could have birthed the whole place and wasn't sure she hadn't. Wondered if some of these were her children. She shook her head and took a long sip.

"You're gonna need boots for the flood of tears and an airplane to get out of here."

The man stuck out his hand. "Ray. You?"

"Toni," she said coolly. "I've written a lot of books."

She started a story in one moment and when words failed, or memory, moved to another. At times she got stuck, like an old LP with a scratch, and Ray would put his hand on her arm, extra weight like the penny she used to tape to the arm of the turntable, and she would pick up somewhere else. Now here, now there—whatever she told, it began in precise detail of acreage and inches. There were underwear drawers stealthily opened and examined, speeches repeated verbatim, and names and nick-names of a few dozen people. And then a strange thing happened.

One moment the front window of the bar was steaming from pots on the stove, the next shattered with bricks. There were cows milling among the tables, then motor cars careening toward the restrooms. The ceiling was the cloudless sky, the fan the first plane over Bainbridge, Georgia, and the floor sticky with slaughterhouse blood. Love and lust and kind-ness and villainy—she was mixing it. Making it up as she went along, her old self would have sneered. A stupid opera.

The bartender turned the music way down, but it stayed on. The music of Mr. Excitement across the decades. At turns gospel, R&B, the blues, jazz. The music behind the clackity clack of the train that was really the rain outside, hammering the awning over the bar door. The music behind Uncle Willie shouting that the plane foretold the end of the world. Behind the shouts and hollering after she and Jackie found the dog.

Me and Jackie was picking berries when we spotted Buss Ward. That was Jackie's dog, you see, and we'd been hunting him for weeks. Now here he was, with a white girl and boy trespassing in Papa's woods. Of course, they didn't see themselves as trespassers. But I expected better of Buss Ward.
You'd of thought a dog raised from a pup would have choked himself on that leash, barking and yapping for Jackie, but the traitor barely sniffed.
"What you done to him?" Jackie wailed.
I recognized the girl. Her family lived on the eastern side of the woods.
"Shut up, tar baby," she told Jackie.
"That's our dog," I said. "That's my brother's dog. And you better watch your mouth.
When they laughed and called more names, I put up my dukes and called out some names too. Jackie jumped in, telling them what Papa would do to them if they didn't return his dog.

"Cut you from stem to stern," he said like a big man. "Shake you from can't see in the morning to can't see at night." I was proud of him.

We couldn't run to the house fast enough and get Papa to do all that fighting we'd threatened. Except that's not how the song went. Them kids went home hollering too and we heard later their daddy come up on Papa's yard with a whole lot of nigger in his mouth, along with his brothers, the sheriff, and a shotgun.

Seemed like we left the South the same week, though it must have been longer. It was a terrible time. Papa moved in with us, and Daddy went north to find work. As our leaving day came closer, I begged Papa to come along.

"That stupid old dog don't care about us." I gave him a thousand more reasons.

Papa listened patiently, nodding his head. And he came close to saying yes a few times, but then Jackie's snotty face would rile him up and he'd shout, "Don't ask me no more, Nell. I ain't leavin!"

When nobody was looking, I'd take me a piece of Jackie and twist it between my fingers and dare him to cry.

A day before neighbors drove us to the train station, Papa announced he was going back to his own house up in the woods.

"Please, Daddy," Mama begged. "It ain't safe."

"Please, Papa," I begged. "Please, Papa, please."

"Got unfinished business," he said, watching Jackie watching him. "I'll be just fine."

I could tell from Mama's face she didn't think so.

Ray bought a round for him and Marjorie, and joining them at the bar, the women paid Marjorie's balance and added a nice tip for Stanley, who kept sweeping away the shells and bringing more peanuts.

They did well to keep their boots on. It was mid-afternoon, under the constant thrum overhead of wooden blades that had forgotten what they were made for and Jackie Wilson going on and on about love, needing love and being loved, when Marjorie's audience, overcome by lassitude, realized they had at last arrived on the segregated end of a train platform and were dripping wet.

The train was late. When it finally pulled in, shaking the platform like it was hungry for wood, stirring its smoke with the dust of that dusty town, there was a crush of hot bodies up the metal stairs and a crush to find seats and sort out children and belongings. Instead of speeding off like trains do in the movies, taking its patient travelers to the greener side of the road, this one crawled like a sick animal. But just as quickly as it came to life, lurching forward so violently that unseated people were thrown about like dolls, it gave a long screeching cry and seemed to die on the tracks.

Something was wrong. Something bad. Crammed into a compartment with a whole other family, smelling the moment Jackie wet himself, and hearing Mama do everything but curse for Nell to close the shade, they were scrambling over knees and suitcases, trying to see who it was, hanging from that tree.

. . .

"It wasn't him, was it?" the bartender asked in a choked voice.

"Naw," said Ray. "He was too smart to take on those bastards himself."

"He must have put up a fight," a woman said softly. "He had a rifle too, didn't he?"

Marjorie twisted around, relieved to see Rosemary. Rosemary here to drive her home. And Linda beside her, still whispering in the scaredy-cat voice that could grate on her nerves. But when she leaned in and her head found a soft shoulder, she was glad. Her little girl was safe and they could go home.

"Was it? Was it Papa?"

Marjorie thought back. It sure looked like Papa. Black man in the kind of white shirt Papa wore to church. About his height too, but maybe all men stretched at the end of a rope look to be the same height. She was just a girl. The baby if Jackie hadn't come along. But she never saw

Papa again after they left so suddenly on the train. Couldn't remember talking to him on the phone either. Or getting a birthday card with a five-dollar bill inside. If she had, she would remember that. Wouldn't she?

. . .

"Toni?"

"Could have been," she said with a breaking sob. "And nobody said nothing."

And that's how the bar understood about the airplane.

ASSEMBLY REQUIRED

The foremost function of a cardboard system is preservation, for if this system fails, no amount of inner cushioning can protect the content who, at this moment, is settling her bottom into the middle one of three egg-shaped cups, the better to be safe. She intuitively fits her legs across two grooves in the cup, allowing her to straddle comfortably into the adjacent one by bending her knees. Her last dose of pain medicine has also helped. As for the third cup, the vacant one behind her, when no other content appears, she decides it's provided as a . . . as a . . . redundancy! Yes, that's the word. A just in case.

She pulls an identical top piece of cushioning over her head and legs, the spacious egg-shape allowing her torso to remain upright, with less pressure on her slipped disc and reducing the chance of breakage in transit. From there the cardboard system takes over. The flaps closing and self-sealing to display an address label (carefully gone over with a black sharpie) and the prepaid sticker.

Somewhere outside the system, in the windup whiz and whir of gadgetry, coupled with the changing tone of darkness inside, something is about to happen. Sure enough, her head is pushed into the back of the cup and feels full and cottony . . . like her blood pressure is off. Too late, she remembers that she hasn't brought along her prescription. Her eyelids close like automatic doors and her sinuses painfully tighten. Departure time.

"I must breathe," she whispers in the dark room of herself. "And hope for the best because the worst is surely behind me."

There is no return address. Instead, she's written "Handle with Care" to disguise its true contents, for high on the list of those whom the world cares little about is a middle-aged Black woman, newly homeless, in a curly wig, stretched out yoga pants and a faded sweatshirt that reads *#1 G-Mom.*

"Breathe," she says out loud as she forces her eyes open.

The unique transparency of the materials allows her to see in every direction as though she were uncushioned, unboxed, but it also increases her disorientation. The system seems to understand and hovers a quarter mile above the neighborhood post office as she carefully counts and re-counts the herd of trucks swathed in security lights out back. On Monday, they will begin their crawl across the city, but none will stop at the box on the tumbledown porch on Mulberry Street where the carrier was informed to hold the mail. Whether she returns or not—and she hopes she doesn't—no bills will pile up and announce to thieves that she has gone away.

Away! Away!

Below her feet, the east side of the city blurs, save for a few recognizable landmarks: the golden arches of McDonald's and the lit pathway of the boulevard splitting the city from the suburbs. When the box makes a slight tilt, as she imagines a bird does when it dips a wing, she has a panoramic view of downtown, an illuminated vision of a bustling nightlife and prosperity you might find on a postcard of a more important city. But was there anywhere more important than here? Her eyes stinging with nostalgia, she quickly reminds herself that her children are women now and that the world has not been kind. Whatever joy she's known has been wrung out of her.

The weight of longing removed, the box lifts quickly, the city lights swallowed into the gray countryside, punctured, like the annual field test she used to have, by sporadic flashes. Homes, cars—no bigger than fireflies.

Higher she goes. Willing it now. Wanting to pump her legs like on a swing set. Wanting to be gone. Faster! Higher! The defined roundness of the planet becoming visible, entire continents as vulnerable as lonely islands . . . whoof! as the box, and she inside, accelerate into thick cloud cover. She cries out, wraps her arms around her chest, as the chalk outlines of Earth wash away. Then WHOOF! Accelerating out of clouds and into black stillness so absolute she wonders if she's moving anymore or stuck in this between place forever.

What have I done? What have I done? What if the rankling thoughts she meant to leave behind return with a vengeance? She scratches under the wig and the twins flit like shadows in the corner of her eyes, their grumbling stomachs persistent as radio waves.

"I must breathe," she reminds herself and is instantly in front of them, a ghost, gesturing towards a bunch of overripe bananas and cereal to tide them over until dinner. Then she exhales them into grown women. Educated, traveling, choosing for themselves. She is *free*—Winter had used that exact word—"Free to do what you please, Mama."

"We have money, Mama. Travel. Enjoy yourself."

Oh, her sweet Summer would give the shirt off her back. They both would. But she won't be a burden to them.

"Breathe."

She gives herself over to the pleasure of being a passenger in a system built for protection and comfort. When thoughts intrude, tells herself, "I've earned this seat by giving the girls as best as anyone might on a troubled planet. Given in double doses what Irene needed and what I was unable to give at the time."

Maximum protection from internal damage. She read it somewhere. Maybe in a book. Maybe on the packaging of the computer the girls gave as a birthday gift.

"Think about yourself, Mama."

"You can go back to school, if you want."

Yes. For a little while she had hunched over the kitchen table, something sweet and appley in the oven, inhaling the world spread at her fingertips. Was taking an online class in human psychology until the recurring thoughts—the dread, the guilt, the certainty that her joy was stolen from Irene, the real Mama, where the girls got their brains from. When her back went out, again, she had to beg the doctor for a prescription, and when that wasn't strong enough, pawn the computer.

"Emails are too complicated," she lied. "I'd rather hear your voices on the phone." Until that number was no longer in service and the neighbor came over, as a favor, to check on her.

"I'm fine, I'm fine. Tell them not to worry. The battery needs replacing."

But now, blackness inside and out the cardboard box, and blacker still, condensed and compacted over and over into the black container of herself, she's excited by the thought of arriving with no baggage. Might she soon be walking about in new shoes and a glowing robe? Or explaining Earth to a crowd of alien scientists?

Higher, deeper. The moon flying up on her right, breathtaking, and gone. She brings her hands to her face. One second terrified that she can't see them, the next delighted.

She is, isn't she? Isn't she fine? Black as she is, invisible against space?

"Look at you!" she shouts as though she were mother of children in the back seat. One with a pinwheel at the open window, the other a book. Proud mother of two fine girls. Girls smart as a whip.

It's warmer or she's feeling warmer. With invisible hands, she removes the invisible wig for a long, hard scratch and shakes out the curls. Then fixing it back, this way and that to set it square, she gives up, contorting her arms to push it into the unoccupied cup behind her. At its soft thud, she laughs, imagining a hairy scowl. But then she hears a second sound, a snap inside her chest, followed by a strange, almost peaceful softening throughout her limbs.

Internal damage, she decides with no great worry, a heart breaking where it was glued and could be again. And so, like most of us, unaware of our own fragile construction until it is too late, the end comes as a surprise: her detached legs slipping off into the farthest cup, her arms falling backwards, senseless, into the wig, and her head flopping between the vee of her torso and collapsed thighs.

How awful to discover, there is no heart in your chest. That what you thought was life was the pull and twist of elastic rigging to simulate animation. How awful to sniff the slightly burnt odor of rubber and realize this narrow existence has reached its end. There is no redundancy. Whoever's doorstep you land on will be disappointed.

THE MOTIVATIONAL SPEAKER

It was the perfect setup and it fell in his lap.

London had a cousin named Gary who worked up at the high school. Teacher with a nice house and a car. One afternoon when he dropped by Gary introduced him to three pretty ladies. Two of them gushed over his baritone voice. *You don't sing? Girls would eat you alive! Move over Barry White!*

Teachers never talked that way in his day. When he was handed a diploma seven years earlier, the principal's handshake felt like a dead snake. And that summer, when he was caught breaking into the shop room, not a single teacher answered the lawyer's request for a character witness. He wound up at the correctional center for nine months as a first-time offender.

A singer? Naw. London had decent carpentry skills, which Gary inflated, always encouraging him to develop his skills and stay out of trouble. "You ain't got to be this," he was quick to say, and that tired line, "You can be anything you set your mind to." Now, just as London was enjoying some love from these fine sisters, he had to go there.

"Wouldn't he be an excellent motivational speaker for our kids?"

Is this what happened to niggas who went to college? He forced himself not to look up at Gary because he didn't want to feel any smaller. Gary was 6'4" and still built like a second baseman. Mutt and Jeff.

"Naw, man. I told you; I'm not interested."

London was seething. At twenty-five, he had spent two and a half years behind bars, a fraction of what most guys he knew had done. The last thing he wanted to do was tell kids to be better people. They'd probably laugh at his voice. When his father was alive, he called London a bullfrog and told him to shut up all the time.

"So, if you don't sing and give speeches, what *do* you do for a living?"

He gave the third lady, Altaira, another look. He didn't go for women with their hair shaved on the sides, but the thick nest of braids at her nape made the style more feminine, as did the loopy blue extensions on top. She looked to be in her late thirties and the prettiest with her smooth, nut-brown face. He tried to see if her hands had the telltale short nails and paint stains of an art teacher, but she kept them stuffed in the pockets of her white smock like a nun. It was sort of sexy.

"Let me guess," she continued with a laugh. "Carpenter?"

"Who told you?" He tipped his chin at Gary, who grinned back. "Just a handyman."

There was an eruption of bells and doors flinging open. The other ladies joined the crowd of students, and Gary, with a wink-wink to catch up later, pounded London's fist and disappeared behind them. Only Altaira stayed. Like a little bird with a crown of blue feathers, she tilted her head as the stampede passed. He wondered if she'd picked up on the double meaning of "handyman."

"Gary's been bragging about the deck you built him. Do you do interiors?"

Now who was flirting? He arched his left eyebrow. "My specialty."

She let the joke go with a smile. "So, how about you come by my house tomorrow for an estimate?"

"Long as it's after five," he said. "I got a job in the afternoon. Where you live?"

He couldn't believe how easy everything was happening. Seamless, until she pulled out a phone to check the calendar.

"Corner of Mulberry and Oak, but that's cutting it close to sunset."

She didn't have to spell it out. He could see pink blotches on her hands. Mulberry Street. Unlike Gary's father, she hadn't moved out. How had he never seen her before?

"Niggas built on the same goddamn place . . . like history don't repeat!" That's what Uncle Cap said before he moved to New York City, leaving the house and bad memories with Aunt Pat.

In the first years after The Fire, Uncle Cap had been optimistic, a steady voice despite the chronic pain from his third-degree burns. After Aunt Fredonia died, he changed. He wasn't cruel like London's father, but not nice anymore either. The reparation money turned him into someone London didn't recognize. Someone who said "nigga." The last time he blew through, he claimed to be sitting pretty with the high rollers.

"Bright lights, big city, London. Come down and stay as long as you like."

The part about "bright lights" was the crack in the bluster and gave London a peek at the scared man underneath. Deep down, every survivor was like Altaira. Hung up on not being caught in the dark.

She bit her lower lip. "Can you make it *at* five?"

The October attack started after sunset, the fires burning all night and into the next morning. London was ten. In his mother's grip, he watched people running from other neighborhoods and ditching their cars. Desperate family and friends, even strangers, rushing the police and fire lines to help. Nowadays, news stories about wildfires and war triggered the memory, the roar of exploding gas tanks and the wind whipped up by the fire. Trapped on the sidelines with the women and babies, pushed farther and farther down Oak, he screamed to be let lose. To save Uncle Cap and Aunt Fredonia and Aunt Pat.

Altaira's breath was ragged. It was cruel, but he took his time pretending to check the calendar on his phone. During daylight hours, Mulberry Street residents seemed normal. Night was different. That's when they locked themselves indoors. That kind of fear could be useful.

"Please. No later than five o'clock."

"Let me see if I can rearrange times with a couple clients."

From the opposite side of the hallway, he spoke into a blank screen and studied her. There was a haunted look about her eyes. You saw it in the others too, people burned out of their homes and scattered ten years before their neighborhood was rebuilt. For him, the place would always be haunted.

The smoke had barely settled when he and his crew, they called themselves The Black Avengers, a mashup of D.C. and Marvel, snuck under police tape onto the incinerated block. He was Black Panther and in charge of assigning names.

"You Blade," he told a skinny, snaggletoothed boy who wanted to join.

"Hell no!" the boy shot back, surprising everyone with his guts. "Blade ain't part of Avengers or Justice League. He ain't part of nothin."

"Then I guess you ain't either."

London still felt a tinge of guilt, and admiration, for the beating the boy took before he ran off. To be a Black Avenger you had to carry some muscle weight or an attitude, and he would have let him join if he'd stayed.

In the early days they'd find people crying and digging through the muddy ash. There wasn't much to find except a few coins, metal bowls, and pots. Then one night Daquan, aka Hulk, alone on the way home, cut across the trackway between Mulberry and the lower street, a stretch of burned trees and shrubs, and got chased by something.

"It was white as milk with wings," he told them. "And big. The moth-erfucker was like a linebacker coming at me."

Afterwards the highlight of night excursions was when someone saw a quick moving line of chalk out the corner of his eye and screamed "Boogeyman!" The short hairs on the back of London's neck tingled as he imagined the creature stalking them like store security, ready to spring when least expected, but London was ready too. Ready to run. He liked the rush of excitement that verged on panic. It felt like traveling back to the night of The Fire. Only this time, with The Black Avengers under his command, he could fight.

"Five it is," he said, strolling over. She lifted the nest of braids and sighed. The doors were closed again, the hallway silent, and still she gave no indication of needing to be somewhere. He didn't look away from her hands quickly enough, and she frowned.

"You married, huh?" he said, having noticed a ring. "Will your husband be there?"

"Felix works second shift, and I don't open the door after dark."

A scaredy cat, London decided. That was good. He would arrive as close to dark as possible, with time to spare for a quick exit.

He planned on 5:10 but it was closer to 5:20 when he entered the block from Bliss Street. Even then he didn't hurry, sauntering past the fancy streetlights which would soon bathe the empty street and yards with a silver glaze. He was just passing Aunt Pat's house, his face hidden inside his black hoodie, when Miss Bullock careened into the opposite driveway like the police were behind her.

"That you London?"

She spoke to him like he was ten and supposed to be doing homework. That was okay because he respected the Bullocks. More than his own family and everybody on this street. He hated to disappoint her.

"You not here to see about your aunt?"

"Not today, Miss Bullock. I got a job."

"Don't take us old folks for granted, London."

"Yes, ma'am."

"Tomorrow is not promised to any of us."

It was 5:30 when he escaped, barely forty minutes before sunset, as he wasted more time outside Altaira's white colonial on the corner. On one of her visits to prison, his mother explained how the terms of reparation were strict: the pillars on the hundred-year-old houses, replaced over time by pressure-treated beams, had to be remade with top-grade materials in their original style. This house must have been the gem of the neighborhood because its round pillars were straight off a plantation. The Big House. But London had read up and wasn't deceived. The terms stipulated the houses meet modern codes and include solar panels and central air.

Now he understood why he hadn't immediately connected Altaira to Mulberry. Her front porch faced Oak Street, so it wasn't technically part of the block. Still, he knew the house well, the decrepit original anyhow, because as kids they believed it was haunted. Old people like Aunt Pat claimed they heard it from old people who heard it from the oldest of the old that the same house had sat on the upper corner for a hundred years. Then one night, no one knew why, it stood on two feet and walked down Mulberry Street. When it reached the corner of Oak, it turned its back and sat down.

And crazy as that story was, Aunt Pat thought it had something to do with a whole street of missing children back in the day.

"Every last one of them fell off the face of the earth."

No kids? He and The Black Avengers fell over each other laughing.

"Laugh all you like," Aunt Pat warned them. "Same thing happen to you if you don't straighten up."

Hopping on the porch like he had found an old friend, London smiled, thinking he too wouldn't mind showing the Mulberry snobs his ass. He knocked on a pillar and didn't see Altaira come to the door, her hands tucked under her armpits.

"You're late."

"But it ain't dark." He patted the sack on his shoulder and talked fast. "Everything's ready. I'm in, I'm out."

Reluctantly she stepped back to let him in, and he gaped at the gleaming wood interior. Carved crown moldings and paned doors that separated the rooms like in a mansion. He knew the doorknobs were crystal from what his mother read in the paper.

"Make you wonder if they didn't set the fire themselves," she joked. But she hadn't laughed.

"You have thirty minutes," Altaira said, leading him through the kitchen—soup simmering on the stove, open purse on the counter, a bag of groceries to put away—and down the cellar steps to a small room, its doorway almost invisible beside the freezer. It was the kind of space you might put an extra toilet, except there was nothing inside except a wooden bench that stretched the length of the far wall. It was handcrafted in dark wood and, despite missing a back support, reminded him of his grandmother's deacon bench, another victim of The Fire. He wondered if this one too had room inside for storage.

"Tut, tut," she said when he tried to lift it.

"So, what you want done?"

"Fireproofing," she said quickly. "I want the entire room fireproofed . . . floor, ceiling, walls."

He hesitated to speak. Too curious not to. "Why you didn't ask for fireproofing when they rebuilt?"

"I want it *extra* fortified. I want a room to survive a goddamn bomb and . . . "

"And?"

"I want to be sure it's done right."

He understood. Who could trust the government after what happened? As impressive as these houses looked on the outside, the builders likely cut corners where it wouldn't be noticed. The foundation, basement. He nodded. More than a few police and firefighters had been complicit, and there were rumors some of the attackers returned as builders and electricians. No telling what mischief they'd done.

"I'll leave you to take measurements," she said. "And hurry, please."

The minute he was alone, his excitement turned into a strange uneasiness. With the door closed, the room was the size of a jail cell, with that same wet dog smell of cement that's absorbed the sweat and piss of trapped and desperate men. And worse. He forced himself to breath. He was smarter now. He wasn't going back to jail. The damp odor meant a leak in the foundation. Shoddy work.

He gave the bench a soft tap. It was hollow alright, but not empty. He wondered if there were guns inside. That's what he would do living on Mulberry Street. Have a gun in every corner of the house and extra ammo in case he had to hole up in a safe, fireproof room for an extended time. Money too. Cash.

He ran his hand along the top for a lock mechanism, pressing every inch. No trick latch but a strange residue. When he rubbed the dark, hairlike strands between his fingertips, they turned to dust. He sniffed his fingers. More of that dog smell.

When she returned, he was squatting with a tape measure in hand. She was wearing an apron.

"You got my estimate?"

He rolled back on the balls of his feet, and setting the tape measure on the bench, picked up his phone.

"The cost of materials spikes this time of year." He poked buttons and frowned. "Let me run these numbers again."

"As long as you hurry."

"You don't have a dog, do you?"

She blinked her eyes. "No," she said after several beats. "We don't like dogs."

It was 5:50. Twenty minutes before sundown. He sat at the kitchen table without being asked and held out his notepad, but her attention had shifted. He watched her check out the window, then open the cellar door a crack, which he couldn't understand, except maybe she was hot from the oven or having an anxiety attack.

When she finally picked up the pad and saw where he'd circled $900, she didn't exactly smile but she audibly exhaled. He suspected this wasn't the first estimate and that the others had gone wildly over. $900 was a safe bet for almost any job. You went higher later, that is if you bothered to do the work.

"If you give me twenty-five percent down," he said. "I'm ready to go."

"How soon?"

"Right away . . . tomorrow . . . before prices go up."

She glanced from her wristwatch to the window. Not for the first time, he thought the terms of reparations should have included more money for therapy. There was a line of sweat between her nose and upper lip.

"I'll need that down payment in order to get the materials. That is if you want top quality and not stuff that'll warp and breach at high temperatures."

"How much did you say?"

He scratched his head. "Two hundred twenty-five. The rest when I finish."

At home she wasn't self-conscious about her pink hands, biting off a hangnail, then moving on to another finger. He was sure that with a gentle arm twisting the deal would be set.

"It sounds fair," she said. "But it's late. You need to come back tomorrow."

He was mystified by the sudden change, then suspicious. A potential client who said "come back tomorrow" usually meant she didn't have the guts to say "no" to his face. He stared down at the table.

"What is it?" she said. "You okay?"

"I'm okay," he said, meeting her eyes. "But I want to be upfront."

"Upfront?"

"What did my cousin tell you about me?"

He already knew the answer. Gary wasn't one to say an ill word against anyone, even if they did deserve it.

She shook her head. "I don't have the—"

"I'll tell you myself."

"Time!"

"Ex-con, but don't worry. Not a violent offender. Not like that."

She edged slightly toward the cellar.

"I don't mean to scare you. If anything, I'm scared."

She looked confused. "Why are you telling me this?"

"Because people can be prejudiced and not give an ex-con a chance." He glanced around the kitchen. The purse was still on the counter. "Afraid we'll rob them."

She folded her arms. "You need to leave."

Shit. He'd fucked up. First arriving too late, then pushing too fast. He had no choice except to plow through. A scared woman might pay to get him out of the house.

"Thing is, I need a guarantee . . . that you're not prejudiced. That we have a deal."

"Your past is your business. But this, this feels rushed and it's turning dark. Dangerous. You need to get going."

"Dangerous? You have no idea how hard these guards are on a man. A Black man."

"You're not hearing me."

He sat up straight like he just might be going after all. But he didn't stand. "Naw, naw. I hear you loud and clear."

"What?"

"After everything that happened, you work with your *good* white people and don't have a problem." He sucked his teeth in disgust. "Then you turn around and don't trust a Black man.'"

"You don't know me."

Hell, he didn't. This bit wasn't acting. It was familiar territory.

"I walk down Mulberry Street and remember The Fire. People scared and homeless and the cops doing nothing, or worse—participating! I get you were outgunned that night. We cried. My family. We watched the news and cried. We got people on this street."

He glanced at her hand gripping the edge of the counter and thought of Uncle Cap's burns and Aunt Pat's depression.

"You were us."

But next he remembered Uncle Cap's desertion with the money and felt hatred inside, disgust, and had half a mind to tell Miss High and Mighty she had an infestation problem. That those "hairs" were probably wood shavings from termites, courtesy of them same *good* white people. He shook his head hard, forcing himself back to the con.

"But after you got your money and new houses, that was it. Revolution over."

"You need to leave *now*."

"Why you didn't go to Washington and demand change?" He stretched out his legs and crossed his arms. "Because you got yours and forgot about the rest of us. We weren't even good enough to be hired for the reconstruction." He put up a hand to shush her. "Only good person come off this street is John Bullock and y'all fine with letting him rot in prison."

The mention of John Bullock hit a nerve. One person sent to prison for The Fire and naturally he was Black. She looked ashamed. "We can talk about this tomorrow."

He glanced at the clock. Seven minutes to sunset. And the joke was on her. He could pull this off, and with a light jog down Oak, sell some weed in the projects before the sun slipped below the horizon.

"As long as we're good with the down payment."

"Twenty-five percent?" She said it like a sneer.

"That's right. Two hundred twenty-five dollars."

She snatched her purse. "I don't carry that much cash."

He counted three twenties in her hand when he heard a baying from the basement and was instantly on his feet.

"The fuck you don't have a dog!"

Whatever breed it was, the thing coming up the steps had speed. Snatching the money, he ran back through the house, so lost in the maze of doors and rooms that instead of exiting through the front porch he stumbled into some sort of coat room. Tripping over shoes and boots, he found a door that led him out, but not to where he intended to be. He ran blind, realizing too late that he had exited onto Mulberry and was heading deeper into the block. Terrified of backtracking in case she let the dog loose, he made a sharp right through somebody's yard and jumped a fence into the trackway where it was already midnight and full of bugs and bats and maybe snakes. His old stomping grounds had regrown into a mini forest.

He never saw it coming. A push from behind. The hold on his neck that pinned him face down in the scrub. No one had tackled him in the game room or shanked him in his cell or made him bend over in the shower. They had come close, but none of that had happened because he was a quick learner and avoided the suffering he would sometimes describe to make ladies feel sorry for him or frightened. Only now, his body flipped back over, he was peeing his pants and shaking uncontrollably. It was Daquan's boogeyman.

"I warned him, Felix," said Altaira, appearing behind the creature's shoulder. A bright penny in its glow. "I kept telling him to leave."

With a low hiss the thing leaned in, letting London see that it was a Black man, his lips and nose intact but his skin chalky. *Felix?* He must have entered the house through the basement. And who wouldn't with that face? How could Altaira stand it? With the thing straddling his chest, he struggled to speak calmly even as words rushed out of him.

"I'm sorry, I'm sorry. The two of you were burned. I'll do one better. I'll do the job at cost."

She scoffed and held up her hands. "This is nothing. Just me, digging in hot embers to find Felix."

Find Felix? London felt a shiver from the thing on top of him. Was it crying? Was it screaming? It made no sound.

"The fire started while he was sleeping. It burned off his skin, but it couldn't kill him."

"Couldn't kill him?" Damn. He was squeaking like a little girl.

"Almost nothing can."

London stared at a pair of fangs inches from his neck, and remembering the bench, felt ice cold in his veins. And yet, cocking a half-melted ear, the thing made no move to hurt him. *It was listening.* A vampire. A black one under white skin. Waiting for instructions.

Forcing his heart to slow down, his vocal muscles to relax, London shifted his attention back to Altaira, but her eyes were wild and unreachable. It was she he understood best, because once upon a time, hating white people, burning with rage, sickened by years of their denial and inaction, he had sought revenge in these same dark woods. Somebody had to pay, and at his signal, his crew would pin down the weakest boy and pummel him.

She didn't care about the money. She didn't even care about him. She wanted revenge too. Someone to feel her pain. He took a deep breath.

"You ain't got to be this," he told the creature, prepared to tell it a thousand times before the sun rose. "Let me break it down for you, Felix. You the *real* goddamn Blade."

WEIGHT

A Black woman who pursues goodness is not rewarded. Her palms, up-turned like Mary's, not filled with light. She is Lady Justice, but blind to the sword in her right hand, she balances the scales in her left like laundry baskets into which she separates the soiled from the clean. While the soiled side is a constant worry of blood and shit, the pile of cleanliness is what topples. The Babylon of pressed and folded goodness what crushes her. What snuffs the light.

Angelica tried to be good, so good that from halfway across a parking lot she could spot a senior shuffling toward a door and hurry ahead to open it. "They making them heavier and heavier!" she'd announce. Or, at the corner market, "They need to put in automatic doors."

Always with a laugh, with a smile. Never winded either, although these days her heart raced a little. The doctor said she needed high blood pressure medicine, but she told him fifty was too young.

"Not for an African American woman your age," he warned. "And weight."

The doctor was among those she didn't extend goodness. *Fuck you*, she thought, with a smile, planning to eat something salty just to spite him. On the way out of the office, she held the door for a white woman in her twenties who didn't say thank you. *And fuck you too*.

The clouds had thickened since she went into the bland brick building for the one o'clock appointment. Suite # 347. The idea of a doctor's office in a suite always gave her a chuckle. As if they were partying together. Her, the doctor, the batty receptionist, and the nurse who looked shitty when Angelica removed her orthopedic shoes before being weighed.

"Not necessary," the nurse said, but Angelica paid her no mind. The one time she didn't remove them, her weight was up five pounds.

Because she refused to take advantage of her handicap sticker, leaving the spots closest to the door for the truly needy, she had a hike to the far end of the lot. First her hip complained, then the gray sky, also unappreciative of her selflessness, opened up and dumped on her like it meant it personally. Shivering as she ran the defrost, mourning her appearance in the mirror, she felt the accumulated weight of all the other times in her life it rained after she spent hours straightening her hair.

The only thing missing was Betty, her older sister, who would enjoy seeing her makeup smeared and hair crinkled. Eight years difference, Betty with the finished edges and a knack for having a hat on hand, an umbrella with a matching bag, and a magician's skill at wrapping a scarf, had grown from a spiteful knee baby to a mocking teenager and was still capable of cruelty. Nowadays there were the cast-off designer clothes she offered Angelica, always two or three sizes too small.

"You're kidding," Betty always said when Angelica declined them. "Didn't we used to be the same size?"

Never. Nor the same income bracket. Angelica moved two hundred miles away, but her sister used social media to boast about her latest promotion and exotic vacations. Despite something mean and unkind shifting in her belly, Angelica would respond with hearts and thumbs-up.

Angelica's belly. Driving out of the lot, she noticed how it nearly touched the steering wheel and recalled the doctor's other warning. That excess belly fat put added strain on the heart. She pooh-poohed his concern but inwardly was terrified because when she listened to her belly at night, she imagined the mound of soil in a Mexican cornfield that erupted into a volcano. Beans and dairy didn't help but she liked her food. Tolerated the churning and gurgling and bloating, although not the cramping that sometimes seized her up. Who knew where things could lead if she didn't get her belly under control? In the middle of planting corn, the farmer dropped his hoe and ran from a towering inferno.

As Angelica maneuvered the rain-covered streets, the wipers barely able to clear the deluge, she admitted to herself that the doctor was probably right. She had to do better. Instead of automatically tuning out Betty, she would get some advice on doing crunches. Maybe join a gym. There was no reason her fifty-eight-year-old sister, her closest relative and beneficiary, should look years younger and outlive her.

Just as she vowed to be good, to be better, the light changed. She put the brakes on too hard and nearly hydroplaned into an Uber driver who flipped her off in his rearview mirror. Rain was normal, if not usually ill-timed, like after the hairdresser or on school picture day, but had it ever rained like this? Following months of drought, buckets. Cats and dogs. Her stomach grumbled. This stuff was biblical. And dangerous. Still shaking from the near collision, she pulled into a McDonald's drive-through.

For people at home, soap operas and talk shows were interrupted with a blast of beeps and an unending band at the bottom of the screen warning about a dangerous storm, winds gusting at upwards of fifty to seventy miles per hour, and the potential for flash flooding. A mile away from McDonald's, on the upper block of Mulberry Street, rain was hitting like an asteroid shower, plowing up the topsoil from Mr. Brown's vegetable garden and grinding loose chunks of concrete and asphalt into pebbles. The uncollected garbage cans raced down a waterfall churning with a basketball, tree limbs, leaf bags, flowerpots, a mangled lounge chair, and a tire. By the time the brunt of that mean black river passed Angelica's house, flattening her streetside flower bed and clogging the grate she conscientiously raked, it wasn't long for it to reach ankle-deep at the stop sign five houses down.

As if sentient, the river hesitated, whirling at the dip in the crossroad before one section charged into the lower block, the other joining a larger river accelerating down the steep decline of Oak Street. Continuing to gather volume and speed with the growing intensity of rain and wind, this massive current hit the bottom of the hill with such force that a manhole cover did exactly what it was designed to do: flew into the air to release the pressure in the pipe below. Nearly three hundred pounds of cast iron, it would have instantly killed anyone passing. Fortunately, the dozen or so people walking or loitering had already fled into the apartments or the businesses on the opposite side, a bakery and convenience store. Unseen, it landed ten yards away hidden by calf-high water that continued to rise.

Angelica thought it a good idea to sit out the storm with her Big Mac. When the rain didn't let up, she changed her mind and decided to get home before it got worse. How much nicer to sip on the supersized Diet Coke with her cat Willow in her lap and her feet up on the ottoman. She proceeded in an easterly direction along Oak Street.

"Why you still living near the projects?" her sister complained. "You got money."

She hated—hated!—the bougie attitude. Her neighborhood was the best she'd ever known. You needed help shoveling or got stuck in the snow? Someone was out of their house, their bed, to help you get to work on time. People paid attention on Mulberry Street. She wouldn't admit this to Betty, but she greeted everyone in kind, and that included the young men who sold weed on the corner. She didn't judge. Her showy garden was a public garden. A gift to her neighborhood. She didn't get mad when kids tried to twist off a few stems for their mothers, sometimes pulling roots and all. She brought out the garden scissors. And though there weren't a lot of businesses left in the area, there was that bakery that made *the brown derby*. A chocolate cake stuffed with fruit and covered in whipped cream. She went in so often, chatting up the friendly baker, that she could tell when his sugar was off by his pale skin (imagine a baker with diabetes!) and name his three children in order of age. She even supported the convenience store where things tended to be overpriced and outdated and everything smelled of tobacco.

The cars ahead of her slowed down as flood water hit the bottom of the hill. She watched the farthest one twist sideways and come to a stop in the middle of the roadway. Almost immediately a pair of arms waved from the driver's side as water quickly rose halfway up the door. Drivers of the other cars managed to avoid the same fate by turning toward the elevated parking lot of the abandoned health center, and Angelica did the same, her relief turning to pride as three men and a woman ran down to join a human chain extending from the bakery. Unconcerned about her hair and clothes, she got out too, then stopped.

In a flash of memory, she was at the beach, gripping strange hands as she shuffled her feet to find a missing child. The water up to her knees, waist, breasts . . . too late to tell someone she couldn't swim. There was a shout from the tower that the boy was found safe, but all the way home Angelica kept thinking that she had been the one drowning.

There looked to be enough strong men and women, but she knew from going to the lake that every hand mattered, so she pushed away her fears and hurried. The water in the lower part of the parking lot soaked her shoes and socks, and as soon as she stepped into the street, the deep current tugged at her pant legs and began fighting her weak hip. But the slight lessening of the wind's fury and the easing of the rain seemed to be good signs. Up ahead she saw the line wobble and hold and a woman, holding the car frame with one hand, reach out the other, dangerously extending her body toward help. In Angelica's head the voices of her neighborhood called out, *We're coming! We're coming!*

She took one brave step and another, confident of the solid street below the water, when suddenly there was nothing under her right foot. Nothing to grab hold of, and in the next instant, only brown water twisting and folding her in half like she were made of cardboard before sucking her out of her shoes and down into the pipes. If the baker hadn't glanced backward, no one would have seen it happen.

Later, while the woman from the car and her rescuers drank coffee to warm up, he stood alone with his vision. A fat Black woman, he had told the 911 operator. About forty, fifty. He couldn't say for sure, because a lot of people came into the shop, but she looked familiar. Someone friendly who might have enjoyed his cakes. She was smiling right before she went under. He could almost swear on that.

TROLL BRIDGE

There was a toll bridge before they put in the highway. You needed a quarter to throw in the basket and a perfect aim. Otherwise you had to wait for the tollkeeper to count out change. That was an option no one wanted, especially late afternoon. If you hit a backup near sundown, you prayed no one ran out of gas or had a flat tire. Carloads of panicked people would try to dash across on foot.

I had five kids and a terrible need to cross every Sunday. Mama still lived in the old neighborhood, cleaning houses to pay off her student loans. She couldn't visit us, and I wouldn't abandon her. My husband threw up his hands, but my kids were great. Age sixteen down to eight-year-old twins, all dressed like me in the old days, going to church. They took turns getting two coins from the roll in the kitchen drawer.

"There's a troll live under the bridge," I reminded them.

If my husband was listening, he'd make a monster face. "Meanest son of a bitch nobody ever saw. Nobody livin'."

The incentive worked until Jimmy said he couldn't find the coming home money in any of his pockets. That day there was a long backup. I had no change in my purse and the smallest bill was the fiver Mama secreted into my pocket, five less than most weeks. Things were getting tight. She usually kept spare change for the kids to run around to the corner store, but she'd only had misshapen apples. Everybody said thank you, all the same, like they were supposed to, except Jimmy. He pouted and upset the day by going missing for ten minutes when we should have been on the road.

"Watch him," Mama warned. "Reminds me of you at that age."

Well, those ten minutes were like the butterfly in South America she used to say shook its wings and sent a tornado spinning into the family farm, two weeks later. I like for her to tell the kids but lately she can't remember details.

"Jimmy, you getting *two* whuppins when we get home." I said this for the tollkeeper's benefit as he slowly counted and also because there was a bulge in Jimmy's cheek.

There was a wet sound on the other side of him, steady as a nursing baby, from where Janie, his twin, turned the pages of her book. Mama's favorite. When my husband tells the kids, "School get you nowhere 'cept in debt," I can see the lights in their eyes dim, except in Janie's.

As the tollkeeper dallied, the tip of the sun appeared in the rearview mirror, and I could feel sweat dripping from my armpits.

"How about you keep the change, sir?"

"What's that?" he hollered. The confusion on his grisly face told me he'd lost count, so the pawing started again. I tried to believe Mama's gift was prescient. At least I hadn't had to use a ten.

The road beyond the tollkeeper was empty. No one going into the city at this hour, and the car ahead had long disappeared. The drivers behind us were flashing their headlights like fireflies when we felt the first vibration. With the second one, the horns began crying and we were jolted by the truck driver tapping us with his bumper. Another strong vibration, and I held my foot hard on the brake, not sure what I would do if the trucker decided to ram us and half wishing he'd push us through the gates.

"Not my fault," I'd tell my husband. "Hit and run."

Beside me, Jimmy was hyperventilating, and Janie rested her book like a butterfly on her lap. I reached across and unknotted her fingers from the door latch, and their stickiness confirmed my suspicions.

"Do something, Ma," Richard pleaded from the backseat.

"Ma!"

"Ma!"

Toni and Margaret, their elbows behind my neck and their knees pressing into my back, were becoming a weepy mess. I thought, "You bunch your Daddy's kids, but you stepped into the world from Mama's bookshelf." Then I took a full moment to love them.

"Hang on, kids!" I said, my voice seeming to come out of the radio. "It can't eat us all."

I caught the trucker's sorrowful eyes in the side mirror, held them as the tollkeeper put change in the drawer and pushed it through. Now the vibration was continuous. The gate went up, and I left it there. Slammed pedal to the floor, hurtling the car across the road, deserted except for mist, white as bones, rising from the river. I didn't stop until the other side.

The truck wasn't behind us. None of the other cars or trucks either. Just toys, the shadows of toys, flying over the sides of the bridge. Behind them the sun melted like a giant Gobstopper on the horizon.

"Don't look," I told the kids as I got out. "Except you." I made Jimmy stand and watch.

He bit hard on his bottom lip, snot and sugar water running down his chin, red and sticky on his best white shirt.

THE CONDUCTOR

Getting off Exit 31 late at night and climbing the steep hill into the east side of the city is a worry. A hundred yards before your ascension, your route intersects with the boulevard flowing along the former channel of the Erie Canal. Night or day, traffic lights here are notoriously long, and at this moment a red light is providential.

In front of you the westward current shimmers with the ambient lights of a gas station and supermarket. Try not to be troubled by the stained roadway ahead, where in bigger cities one would find a pedestrian cross-walk. The red. It might be a reflection from the traffic light or residue of an accident, a frequent occurrence at this spot, for the town planners will not budget crosswalks for another decade. The red. It's impossible to tell its origin from inside your vehicle, and you have somewhere to be, so concentrate on what's to your right and at the triangular island which cuts between you and the eastward flow. The oasis for panhandlers. The workers in this ancient industry are gone, and at this late hour tucked under bridges or sheltering at the shelter. Your eyes seize on what is left behind: the scattered water bottles glittering like seashells.

Now blink, if you must, blink away that tick, that prick, that red-white-blue flickering flick of the disembodied arm of Paul Bunyan, that most American of American folk heroes, ceaselessly chopping his ax above the dark supermarket. Not much time. Quickly. Focus ahead. Shift your eyes to the left. And squint. Just there, for you won't believe me otherwise. You must see for yourself. In the parking lot of a former bike shop. Across from the all-night McDonald's. Zombies.

The light won't stay red forever, so you must decide. Now. To continue straight or find a different crossing. The choice is not always available. If you're in a hurry, for instance, or neurotically connected to your GPS.

If you do go straight and the zombies run like deer into your headlights, you face a quandary. Hit them square on and doom yourself to eternity or lay on the horn in bowel-loosening terror until they grow bored of battering the thin wall of metal between you and them. Very rarely a cop will come out of McDonald's. Cops aren't any braver around zombies than anyone else, so you shouldn't expect Rambo. No matter. This particular band has an aversion to police. At the least scent, they wave their arms like oily seabirds and scatter.

You're in luck. Aside from yourself, there are two others attentive to the streets tonight.

"Brothers and sisters," a woman calls from the top of the hill. "Take heart!"

You missed the other. In his dark dress coat and top hat, he is as much a part of the island as the litter and directional arrows. Slouched in a sitting position, the old man dozes on his cane, wheezing and snoring in time with Old Paul, still chopping away at the night. There is a ring of keys attached to the lanyard at his waist. "A ring to every lock in the world," he'd proclaim if you met him jingling down the aisle of public transport. At his feet is a square of cardboard that has survived the heat of yesterday morning, followed by the torrential rain of the afternoon. In six months it will survive the snow, for it's sturdy as stone, his sign, and etched with a single word in permanent marker: *hope.*

Some history is needed. First, about the businesses that root below the boulevard, spreading fast as kudzu, although the occupants come and go, reeling in passersby as easily as fishing in April. It hasn't always been all money-money around here. A thousand years before the drive-through restaurants and adult clubs, this land belonged to the Onondagas (still does), one of the five nations of the Haudenosaunee (Iroquois) Confederacy, brought together by the Peacemaker. The "discovery" of salt around 1654 by French missionary Father Simon Le Moyne was eventually superseded by the establishment of English colonies. By 1825, America was a free and independent country and the Erie Canal, a 363-mile system of locks that stretched from Albany to Buffalo, a glowing example of the young nation's supremacy. Some might add, its inevitability. The system transported goods as well as people, some of whom were escaping bondage in the southern states. That's the next part of the history.

The city and surrounding area became an important and storied stop along the Underground Railroad. A newspaper of the time called it "a hotbed of abolitionist activity." After 1850, with the passage of The Fugitive Slave Act, and the criminalization of aiding and abetting escape, the goal wasn't simply to reach North but to reach Canada. One notable stop along The Railroad was the house of former slave and firebrand Reverend Jermain Wesley Loguen, "The Lord bless him," as the passengers used to say. Despite threats to life and freedom, he may as well have placed an actual welcome mat on the porch, for he publicly chided his neighbors to look out for the least of these.

Nowadays houses across this region appear on the National Register of Historic Places. Homes such as those designed by famed architect Ward Wellington Ward. As fine as they are, these houses are far less significant than that of the good Reverend's, but it was his that was torn down in the late twentieth century. His great wooden door with its iron knocker, loud enough to get Heaven's attention, replaced with an automatic door into a chain pharmacy. His good and firm handshake supplanted by the cold eye of the manager.

There is so much we manage to miss as we buy our Kleenex and lottery tickets. While we hold up the line counting the pills for our bad backs and sciatica because the pharmacist looks shifty. So much history that is not all behind us.

If you stop measuring in miles, you can glimpse the true distance crossed to reach the Loguen Stop from the farthest reaches of bondage. But can you hear the disappointment? See the arm waving of the unhappy souls? Feet weaving in exhaustion? The madness caused by prolonged hunger and fear? You can if your eyes are sharp enough. If you unwind your car window and listen.

"But you must be kidding," I hear you say. "This is nothing but noise wrapped in silence."

A few visual iterations of the zombie language might prove useful. Take a pen from the glove box and spell a dying man's cry for his mother and her answer from the grave. Conjugate the scream of a child being tasered in the next classroom. Parse out the separation of neck from noose, flesh from bone.

But perhaps the exercise above is too cruel, too difficult. Too precise. Perhaps you prefer a more speculative approach. So instead consider questions the zombies might be asking each other and anyone listening. (You are still listening, aren't you?) Where is the door we were promised? Where are the ringing words of Loguen and his friend Frederick (his own home burned to the ground in 1872)? Where is our King?

In the absence of answers, the digestion of the accidental traveler or the occasional do-gooder offering socks and water is scarce recompense for the zombies' profound disappointment. Noise wrapped in silence, or silence wrapped in noise. Does it matter?

There isn't much to add, though I urge you to talk to the woman piloting a cardboard ship to these strange shores. She wears a dress and head wrap so white they would shame a ghost, but it is her feet she is most proud of. Those ashy, unashamed mud mashers visible as she disembarks, bent at the waist. Nearly L-shaped from her long confinement.

"This way," she whispers, shooing zombies under the noses of the cops and the staff of the all-night McDonald's. "This way," across the eastward flowing current of the boulevard. "This way from the hurt and hunger of a cruel world."

She could be mistaken for one of those kindly, grandmotherly types, forever underestimated, whose insistence on being understood and obeyed for one's own good, means she shall always be so. But she is here as much for herself as for anyone. Listen to the slap of bare feet as she leads the tired band to the island. Feet she has earned. Feet so rooted to this earth and hope that her spine straightens. She calls out a god from his slumber.

MR. BROWN

Mr. Brown was hoping for something finer than the car he managed to wave down. Truth was there weren't many luxury cars on Mulberry Street anymore. Now and then a Cadillac with out-of-state plates would squeeze into someone's driveway, but nowadays caddies usually meant bad news. The young couple from the end of the street pulled over in their battered Capri.

"Everything okay?" the woman asked from the passenger side.

Mr. Brown disliked how the driver continued to stare ahead, a slight frown on his face. It was obvious he hadn't wanted to pull over.

"Need a ride to the south side," he hollered from halfway down the steep cement steps of his house.

The woman said something to the driver then said that it was no problem. "You just tell us how to get there."

Mr. Brown moved slowly. He rubbed his hands together and patted the pockets of his suit jacket, shiny with age. The driver didn't protest when he helped himself into the back seat. Didn't say peep when a dog stuck his head over the front seat and barked.

"Sorry," the woman said. "He's not dangerous."

Mr. Brown slipped a hand in his pocket. "You keep a good hold on that dog," he said like he didn't believe her.

The woman smiled anyhow. "Wherever you're going, we can take you." She turned to the driver. "Right? We got time. We got all the time in the world."

The old man grunted, not taking his eye off the dog, and the dog not taking his eye off him. He'd had a dog once. It was before his family moved up from Florida and long before he married Gracie. Best dog in the world until he wasn't.

"What's the address?" the woman said. "I can put it in my GPS."

"No address," Mr. Brown snapped. "Listen up good. Turn right at the end of the street."

The driver chuckled to himself. He gave the woman the side eye and something shifted in the car. At the stop sign, the man let the dog crawl in his lap and rubbed his head. Then he waited, being extra careful that nothing was coming in either direction, before he turned. The gesture seemed full of meaning. Like he was communicating something to the back seat. This had not been his idea, but he would see it through. Get Mr. Brown to his destination in one piece. But he didn't speak and that didn't sit well with Mr. Brown who had a half mind to get out.

"Didn't he say the south side?" the woman asked the driver, her voice tight. "If he did, we ought to take the highway."

"Turn right!" Mr. Brown shouted, and the driver hit the brake and made a wide turn. He lifted his hand to a driver forced to make room.

The woman smiled. Satisfied. It was a turn in the direction of the highway. But when they got to the stop sign and should have crossed Oak, Mr. Brown said, "Right. Take a right."

"But—"

Whatever the woman intended to say, preempted by her husband's eagerness to proceed as directed, it was replaced by a *hmpf* loud enough to make Mr. Brown chuckle.

"Thank you, sir," he told the man, who nodded respectfully, but when he repeated, "turn right," the driver came to a complete stop before making another awkward maneuver. They were back on Mulberry Street.

The driver glanced at the woman and a deep silence hung between them. Only the dog spoke. A hum of recognition. Happy to be closer to home, his bowl, his bed. It stood and wagged its tail.

"You tell us how to go," the woman told Mr. Brown. And to the man, "Go slow, Roy."

He was glad she'd stopped making suggestions about the route. He didn't trust people who talked too much.

"You can drop me at the yellow house there. With the steps."

The man pulled the car to the side of the street and shut it off. He got out and went around to open the door for Mr. Brown who couldn't find the inside latch. "This is more like it," Mr. Brown thought to himself. "Door-to-door service." It was a low riding car and so he let the man help him up. Escort him like a celebrity. This was the way he'd wanted to be treated his whole life. A gentleman. A man of means. A lion of his community.

Jackie Wilson Brown. A schoolteacher liked to sing out his name when she called the roll and watch him hide a grin in his hand. "A born showstopper."

And not a fool, for when the man didn't let go, held his arm in a proprietary grip that would have terrified a small woman, Mr. Brown shook himself loose and practically marched. His back straight. His chin high. His hip bones shaped like pistols under the low pockets of his jacket.

JOHN AND THE DEVIL

When the Devil flew down Mulberry in an extra wide truck with seating for a small militia and a silver gun vault prettier than most coffins, John about swallowed his cigarette. When the Devil showed his ass a second time, sashaying around the corner like Miss Scarlet in a huff, he took chase.

You can read the details online. Crossing and recrossing city streets, the two vehicles managed to make it to the highway where they reached speeds topping one hundred miles per hour. Looked like the Devil wanted to race John to the Canadian line. Full of ambition, he forgot to slow down on the exit ramp to the NYS Thruway West and went airborne, while John, downshifting his six-year-old Malibu, was saved by the guardrail. He heard an EMT say the other driver wasn't so lucky and was still trying to say "Fuck that motherfucker" through a busted jaw as the police handcuffed him to the hospital bed. Hell cheered a minute then got back to business.

The neighbors were divided. Some said John did right to stand up for himself, for the neighborhood; others that he'd probably made things worse. Up and down the street, old folks got to rearguing the election of the first Black president.

"I like him," said Miss Jenkins, the oldest of the old, then repeated her resistance to then-candidate Obama. "But y'all too young to have seen the Devil up close. He don't like to lose."

Her opinion, which had once sounded like heresy, was proven right by a mounting pile of Black bodies. Jim Crow was feasting, and the louder people protested, the hungrier he got.

Mrs. Jenkins, the oldest of the old the first time she voted for Obama, pointed to the sky like her uncle had in 1914, seeing a plane for the first time.

"End Time!" she shouted over and over from her porch.

"What's that you say?" a little boy named London asked. His head full of superhero missions, he was on his way to his Aunt Pat's for lunch. While most people crossed the street when Miss Jenkins got into one of her states, arguing with invisible people, London considered her a valuable source of intel.

"Ain't what I say, chile. It's what I see. Silver Squitas, big as crows, buzzing over my rhododendron."

London carried the news like the town crier, but everyone was tired of his lies. That, plus the fact a sense of doom was hanging over the country like pea soup, and now this trouble on Mulberry, made folks shrug at the warning of silver Squitas big as crows. Long as the Earth was turning and the clock was ticking, they had work that added up to more than twenty-four hours a day.

That's why a week after Miss Jenkins's announcement, when The End Time arrived, Mulberry Street was like a child playing with a toy gun in the park, a boy, all up in his music, walking home from the corner store, a man jogging/driving/drinking coffee, a woman sleeping in her bed. In other words, it still managed to be surprised.

By the time this exposé was published in a national newspaper, four years of untreated trauma had passed like forty:

Hoping to spark a race war, white supremacists had been planning the attack for months. . . . An hour before sundown, drones sprayed accelerants on houses and outbuildings. Next, moving in tandem through back yards on both sides of the street, white men wearing dark masks ignited fires that quickly accelerated . . . .

. . . subsequent investigation uncovered a few infiltrators among the first responders. As the evening sky became thick with black smoke, some firefighters pointed their hoses into the street while, under the direction of a now

deceased police captain, victims, as well as others running into the confla-gration to help, were misidentified as perpetrators and arrested. . . . The vast majority of these charges were later dropped . . .

Too bad Black people don't live in the future. Where they live, John Bullock, or someone like him, is in a courtroom right now. In John's case, the prosecutor is showing irrefutable evidence that his pursuit of the truck driver, leading to the latter's "tragic" death, was the first stage in a calculated plan to trigger an all-out war with the police.

"I urge you, The Jury, to look deeply under the surface of this man's life."

Look. A recurring monthly donation to something called Bail Relief Fund. *Look.* A black T-shirt he wore to a rally to defund the police. *Look.* A Google search of "Molotov cocktail." *Look.* A propensity to call white people "devils." *Look.* Heated arguments at work that frequently became "racialized" by the defendant. *Look.* A leader of Antifa bent on inciting a civil war.

It was a lot to take in, and whenever he could, John risked a glance at his friends Peetie and Gary, who didn't miss a day of court. Peetie cried a lot, while Gary looked frozen. The only time John had been in charge of anything, the three of them were running a blood drive in high school. *Antifa?* He had to have his lawyer explain it to him.

But bottom line, the neighborhood was gone. Burned to the ground. And Mama, a row ahead of Gary, had scars he'd seen up close during their brief visits. She always laid hands on the glass window, thanking God for saving him in the car crash.

"He got bigger plans for you, John Bullock. You just don't know what they are yet."

And whether he professed his guilt-ridden heart or hid it behind a face swollen with grief and self-hatred or from an assault, she somehow reached *through* the glass, taking it up easy as a lump of dough and rolled and pulled and stretched and reformed it with her love and intelligence.

"Ma, I can't stand to think about you out there, homeless."

"Homeless? How you think we come up here with just the clothes on our backs? We know how to survive."

Oh, his Mama was steel. A shield and sword.

"Johnny, son, never give up on the power of God and prayer and your people."

He wanted to believe her, to believe in himself, but being locked up without books—good books—and other diversions of the mind was hard. Once the Devil had a hold of him, John was lost.

He was numb when a formula was worked out that gave him twenty to thirty years maximum. Silent with self-hatred. If he'd watched the news or seen a paper, he would have wanted to hug the state senator who opined, "Criminals with this level of disregard for property and human life are no better than an animal. Put him in a hole!"

That line didn't sit well with a lot of people and caused the senator some trouble, but it got him some votes too. John would have voted for him. And when he discovered solitary confinement, a hole within a hole, it suited him even better. He didn't tap-tap or dig an escape tunnel like the Count of Monte Cristo. Didn't replay the morning of the incident over and over in his mind and regret it. Didn't cry. He sat cross-legged like Indian yogis he'd read about and willed himself to die.

But something inside John Bullock resisted, for the back of his throat dripped with pot likker. He sat and kept sitting for fifteen years until a new governor gave him a full pardon he didn't want. When he stood and walked, he was bowlegged as Popeye.

On the day of his release, he took his sack of belongings and headed north. He had enough money in his threadbare wallet to take a bus with plenty of stops. Plenty of time to study the world outside without needing to talk to anyone. He'd read about climate change before he went in and was grateful there was still air to breathe . . . and trees. He was glad they hadn't been swept away by tornadoes. He said hallelujah more than a few times, for the road between prison and home showed him that the impossible had been possible. The country had been burning when he went away—wildfires, cities, tempers—but life had kept on. Now he had to do his part.

"Lord!" he prayed in the middle of the Catskills. "Get me to Mulberry Street so that I may atone for its destruction."

Afterwards he intended to keep traveling until he reached the North Pole. He figured he'd build a fire under a tree like a man in a story he remembered from high school. When the fire got hot enough, a clump of snow would fall from an overhanging branch and snuff it out and he'd get hypothermia. The English teacher said dying in the snow was easy as falling asleep, and though John knew he didn't deserve an easy death, he didn't have the guts to jump from an overpass or the patience to put a belt around his neck and hang from a doorknob.

Had Mulberry Street moved? Picked itself up like the house that walked down the block? He lost his bearings and couldn't find it for hours. For one thing, the whole city was different. More black and brown people than he remembered. And not too shabby either. Looked like they was just about running the place. Doing the construction work, delivering mail. According to the signage, running for mayor and judge, and representative of this and that. Running for *reelection*!

There were messages on the lawns too. Positive ones like he used to see in school. *You matter! Don't give up!* "Ha-ha," he told himself. "In your dreams, John Bullock."

. . . then here he is. At the bottom of the block, where Mulberry crosses Oak. It's midnight and here is the house he was dreaming about last night. The one that had its reasons for turning its back on Mulberry Street. It remained a crooked wreck no matter how many times someone jacked the porch.

It seems to have turned again. And if he hadn't remembered the lantern cutouts in the upstairs window frames, like the house in *The Amityville Horror*, he wouldn't have recognized it at all because the porch is finally straight. But has it always had round pillars or is the fresh coat of white paint, brilliant under the working streetlamp, playing games with his eyes? He throws off his cigarette and steps closer. There are flowerpots on the porch, pretty hanging ones, and two sets of French doors that must lead into the living room where the gray light of television flickers through lace curtains. When he slows his breathing, he hears a rumble of laughter under a higher-pitched note. A summer night with a breeze, the windows open, the crickets in the grass singing with the kind of everyday joy he and his grandmother had shared.

Stepping into the center of the street he casts his eyes down the evenly spaced lampposts. What magic is this? They are the old-fashioned kind, the ones that need a little lamplighter with a long pole. As far as he can see, their soft halos cast a prettiness over the neighborhood that help him imagine, as he did as a boy, the plan of the original builders. The splendor.

So pretty and peaceful . . . and strangely deserted for a Saturday night. Deciding midnight is too cowardly an hour, he postpones his atonement for eleven o'clock on the Sabbath. Mama will be at church.

This time he enters from the top of the block. Where Mulberry meets Bliss.

His heart breaks. By day it is clear that the lamplight had been no trick. Mulberry Street is gone. Peetie's front porch where they drank beer after work, Gary's pocked driveway with a basketball net over the garage, Miss Jenkins's roses—all gone, like a magic wand has transformed the ramshackle houses into ones nicer than where they trick-or-treated. It looks like the Devil wins. Cleared the land for newcomers. Gentrifiers. From the solar panels covering the roofs, he smells a future where Black people don't live.

To get here today, John passed a house with garbage out front, a broken rake in the pile of discards. Now he backtracks, retrieving it as a disguise. When he reaches the middle of the block, where his grandmother's blue house used to be, he leans into the rake like it's a shepherd's crook, and taking a knee, bows his head.

"Forgive me, Mama, for what I've done."

"What you've done"?

He keeps his eyes closed, expecting a white mob to set upon him. Hold him until the police come and return him to the hole where so many times he wished to die. Unless they shoot him dead right here, claiming he resisted arrest. He puts a hand purposefully into his pocket and opens his eyes to his executioners. Except there is no mob. Just a grey-haired man staring back. A face both familiar and not familiar.

"Damn, Peetie. You got old."

"And happy brother. Happy to see you."

John stares at Peetie's empty hands, then catching himself, looks away. His friend's hands and forearms are pure white.

"What kind of work you do here?"

"Fool. I live here. And so do your grandma."

John barely notices his friend talking low and careful, as if he's dealing with a child. He lets himself be pulled to his feet or rather reeled in like the fish they used to catch off Caughdenoy Road. Before solitaire, John burned his hand working in the kitchen. It hurt and blistered but the skin came back the same color. He's ashamed to meet Peetie's eyes because these white hands frighten him, bring back the nightmares of the hole. White hands he has no strength to escape. If his friend notices, he doesn't show it.

"We been waitin' on you, hero," he says when he has John steady in his arms.

Hero? Is he dreaming? Here's Mama gliding down from the porch in front of him, dressed head- to-toe in white like she's heading for the crossroads instead of fixing to take him into her arms and cry. They are both crying and when they've cried themselves out, the doors of other houses open and neighbors, even the little ones, eating John up with their round eyes, file past, one by one, pat-patting his arm like he's stretched out in a coffin. Only he's alive, if you count being held between your elderly Mama and your old friend.

He recognizes a few faces, is baffled by others. In either case, each person says their name out loud like it's being recorded into a book.

"Altaira," says a pretty woman, about forty-five, who he's sure he'd remember if they'd ever met. What he first thought was a shirt are inter- locked tattoos on her arms and chest. "I heard you like banana pudding."

The last one is an old woman who embraces him for the longest time.

"Who was that?" he whispers to Mama.

"You remember Miss Pat. She helped me write an appeal letter every time you came up for parole."

He drops his face in shame. He'd blown his hearings by lying to the panel when he said he had no remorse.

"Miss Pat told us you'd be coming today," Peetie says, and John won- ders if he isn't dreaming . . . or dead.

They let his grandma doctor on him for six days and when he rises on the following Sunday, they've returned with enough food and drink for a city. Everyone except Miss Pat, although her nephew, his old friend Gary, carries a sweet potato pie she baked the night before.

"She'll be alright," he assures everyone. "Aunt Pat old as Mulberry Street and just as tough. I wish my cousin London was here though. You remember that tagalong."

John has a vague memory of a big-headed boy wanting an autograph after the championship game, senior year, and asks after him cautiously, in case he's dead.

"Where he at?"

Gary pulls him aside to speak privately.

"You turned his life around."

"Me?"

"He did time himself and kept messing up. Then about a year ago he got a good-paying job at the casino. Works the graveyard shift and sleeps all day."

"How I have anything to do with that?"

"Don't you get it, man? You're a hero, an inspiration. You stood up for the neighborhood and paid the price."

"I was a fool."

"Naw. You're a hero. Don't tell him I told you, but he got your name inked on his back."

John is speechless.

"What can I fix you, Johnny?" Mama calls out. She's turning chicken on the grill, and at seventy still looks like a Hollywood star. But there are lines around her eyes, and John knows she cried every day he was gone and is on the verge of crying right now, same as him. He focuses on the gentle strokes of sauce she adds to the meat, and slowly, with great effort, pulls his face muscles into a smile the neighborhood will warm its hands over when winter returns. Way down at the back of his throat he's tasting those years in solitaire and his mouth waters.

"You listening, Johnny?"

"Greens," he says, then grins at his neighbors. Cheek by jowl, they're crowding picnic tables set end-to-end, all talk of heroes lost between bites. "If any left, that is."

Of course there is, John Bullock. There's plenty for everyone. And anyhow, she's set a plate aside, just in case.

THE END

175

ACKNOWLEDGEMENTS

Thank you, Kimbilio—founders, fellows, instructors, and supporters — and to SMU, for "the safe haven" where these stories were born. Thank you, Diana Napier and David Haynes, for working tirelessly to make a wider way for Black fiction to be created, then read and heard. I'm deeply grateful to Martha Rhodes, Ryan Murphy, Hannah Matheson, Sally Ball, and everyone at Four Way Books for shepherding the book to completion, and to David Haynes and Nancy Koerbel for your thoughtful and gentle editing. Carolyn Ferrell, judge of the Kimbilio National Fiction Prize, I owe you much gratitude, not just for choosing, but for encouraging and inspiring me with your soaring prose. Flowers for Rosalyn Story, Ravi Howard, and Lyndsey Ellis, as well, for being among the first readers of this collection. As I wrote and edited, I read your lovely books and found signs everywhere that said, "Right this way." I appreciate you, Joan Bryant, and our long neighborhood walks, laughing under our masks as the collection took form. You never batted an eye at the fantastical world. And thank you, Rajeswari Mohan, for telling me honestly, back in the eighties, that Black stories would always be a hard sell, then demonstrating through your brilliant scholarship, like Joan's, that always ain't forever. A bouquet for Tara Masih, friend, supporter, sometime-mentor, for being the first to edit and publish a flash in *Riding the Dangerous Wind—A Folio of Flash Fiction*. I appreciate how you seek ways to include me and other women in your own success. Thank you, Marjorie Altman Tesser, Cindy Veach, and Jennifer Martelli of *Mom Egg Review* for publication and nomination of work to *Best Small Fictions*

2021 and to Sonder Press and guest editor Rion Amilcar Scott, world builder extraordinaire, for inclusion. Early publication of stories was a blessing and impetus to keep working, so more flowers for Duriel E. Harris and Tara A. Reeser of *Obsidian: Literature & Arts in the African Diaspora*, Whitney Cooper and guest editor Lyrae Van Clief-Stefanon for the "Black Lives Matter" section of *Jelly Bucket*, and Ianna A. Small at *midnight & indigo: Nineteen Speculative Stories by Black Women Writers*. I cherish my family of spoken word poets, prose writers, and good souls at *great weather for MEDIA*. Jane Ormerod, Thomas Fucaloro, David Lawton, Lyndsey Ellis, George Wallace, and Pete Darrell, you remind us to read and listen to others, to be inclusive, and to grow our art communities with both words and actions. Yes, I have wonderful friends. Thank you Agatha Devore for candy bars and for championing Black everything, and Amy Zamkoff and Sidney Manes for food and laughter and a sense of justice that ought to shake the world straight. Patrick Lawler, your friendship is a constant light, and Natalie Reeves you inspire me. I love you Onie Butler, Gloria Wiggins, Rita Kelley, Raquel McLaughlin, Rennie and Martha McLaughin, and FAMFAM. Mulberry Street is far from home, but you'll recognize flashes in its houses and people and in the beautiful cover by Aunt Rita. To be loved like that! Thank you, Jackie Wilson, for saying it much better with music, and to Toni Morrison, for that bench on the moon. Raina Kelley, your vision for Andscape, an endless future of Black possibilites, will keep me writing, God willing, to a ripe old age. Ashe.

I love you dearly, my quarantine bubble: Miles, Angela, Leo, Sterling, Stephanie, and Asher Slechta. You are the kindest, lovingest family a woman could be blessed with. Thank you, Matej, for this life we've created together. I love you.

Two final notes of gratitude. First, to Rivka Agarwal, MD for the emergency surgery in the middle of edits and your hug that meant that work could be finished. And lastly to Rachel Gullotta. Your smile behind the camera helped me start to see myself whole again.

ABOUT THE AUTHOR

Mary McLaughlin Slechta grew up in a world carved out of rural Connecticut by southern African-Americans and Jamaicans. She received her Bachelor's and Master's Degrees in English from The University of Connecticut and Syracuse University, respectively. She is author of a chooseable path book, *The Spoonmaker's Diamond* (Night Owl Press), and a poetry collection, *Wreckage on a Watery Moon* (FootHills). She has also published a chapbook with FootHills and two collaborative chapbooks with the artist Rita Kelley (Feral Press). Her recent work appears in many journals and anthologies, including *Mom Egg Review, Rattle, jelly bucket, Obsidian: Literature and Arts in the African Diaspora, midnight & indigo,* and *The Best Small Fictions 2021.* A multiple Pushcart nominee and recipient of the Charlotte and Isidor Paiewonsky Prize from *The Caribbean Writer,* she was a two-time poet-in-residence at the Chautauqua Institution and is a Kimbilio Fellow. She lives in Syracuse, NY, with her husband and extended family and stays busy year-round as an editor with *great weather for MEDIA.*

PUBLICATION OF THIS BOOK WAS MADE POSSIBLE
BY GRANTS AND DONATIONS. WE ARE ALSO GRATEFUL
TO THOSE INDIVIDUALS WHO PARTICIPATED IN
OUR BUILD A BOOK PROGRAM. THEY ARE:

Anonymous (14), Abby Wender and Rohan Weerasinghe, Robert
Abrams, Michael Ansara, Kathy Aponick, Arthur Sze & Carol Moldaw,
Jean Ball, Sally Ball, Clayre Benzadon, Adrian Blevins, Laurel Blossom,
Adam Bohannon, Betsy Bonner, Patricia Bottomley, Lee Briccetti,
Joel Brouwer, Susan Buttenwieser, Anthony Cappo, Paul and Brandy
Carlson, Dan Clarke, Mark Conway, Elinor Cramer, Kwame Dawes,
Michael Anna de Armas, John Del Peschio, Brian Komei Dempster,
Rosalynde Vas Dias, Patrick Donnelly, Lynn Emanuel, Blas Falconer,
Jennifer Franklin, John Gallaher, Reginald Gibbons, Rebecca Kaiser
Gibson, Dorothy Tapper Goldman, Julia Guez, Naomi Guttman and
Jonathan Mead, Forrest Hamer, Luke Hankins, Yona Harvey, KT Herr,
Karen Hildebrand, Carlie Hoffman, Glenna Horton, Thomas and
Autumn Howard, Catherine Hoyser, Elizabeth Jackson, Linda Susan
Jackson, Jessica Jacobs and Nickole Brown, Lee Jenkins, Elizabeth
Kanell, Nancy Kassell, Maeve Kinkead, Victoria Korth, Brett Lauer
and Gretchen Scott, Howard Levy, Margaree Little, Sara London and
Dean Albarelli, Tariq Luthun, Myra Malkin, Martha Rhodes & Jean
Brunel, Louise Mathias, Victoria McCoy, Lupe Mendez, Michael and
Nancy Murphy, Kimberly Nunes, Susan Okie and Walter Weiss, Owen
Lewis and Susan Ennis, Cathy McArthur Palermo, Veronica Patterson,
Jill Pearlman, Marcia and Chris Pelletiere, Sam Perkins, Susan Peters
and Morgan Driscoll, Maya Pindyck, Megan Pinto, Kevin Prufer, Paula
Rhodes, Louise Riemer, Peter and Jill Schireson, Rob Schlegel, Yoana
Setzer, Soraya Shalforoosh, Mary Slechta, Diane Souvaine, Barbara
Spark, Catherine Stearns, Jacob Strautmann, Yerra Sugarman, Marjorie
and Lew Tesser, Dorothy Thomas, Rushi Vyas, Martha Webster and
Robert Fuentes, Rachel Weintraub and Allston James, Monica Youn